MURDER IN THE VALLEY OF THE HEART'S DELIGHT

Murder in the Valley of the Heart's Delight

A Mobfoolery Mystery

DONNA LANE

J. Channing

Red Team Ink (DBA) of Zealot Solutions Idaho

Dedication

I got the idea for this story as I drove home from my folks' house and saw a lone turkey vulture circling in the sky. I'd just spent part of the day looking after my father, who was in the early stages of his battle with Lewy body dementia. One life starting anew, another drawing to a close. Both of us circling as we awaited whatever was to come.

I dedicate this book to my children, my sisters, my parents, and my good friend who listened to my crazy ideas as I wrote this story. Some have walked on since that afternoon, no longer with me in this space and time. But I hope I've honored you all as I've written this tale of families and feuds, of greed and grief, of love and loss.

Love,
DL

Red Team Ink
DBA of Zealot Solutions, Idaho LLC
9480 River Beach Lane
Garden City, ID 83714
Copyright © 2022

All rights reserved. Without limiting the rights under the copyright reserved above, no part of this publication may be reproduced, stored in, or introduced into a retrieval system, or transmitted in any form or by any means (electronic, mechanical, photocopying, recording, or otherwise) without prior written permission.

This is a work of fiction. Names, characters, businesses, places, events, and incidents are either the products of the author's imagination or used in a fictitious manner. Any resemblance to actual persons, living or dead, or actual events is purely coincidental.

For permission requests or information about discounts for special bulk purchases please contact: redteamink@gmail.com. Substantial discounts on bulk orders are available to corporations, professional associations, and small businesses.

Printed in The United States of America
Print Book ISBN: 978-1-0880-6395-8
E-Book ISBN: 978-1-0880-6402-3
Title: Murder in the Valley of the Heart's Delight
Description: First Edition
Cover design by Donna Lane

| 1 |

Soaring in concentric circles, the turkey vulture's ebony wings unfurled against the cloudless June sky to the east. Eufrasio Volpe looked up from his spot on the bocce ball court, tucked into the end of his property at Lion Creek Lane. It overlooked Bel Monte Boulevard, the main path in and out of town before the freeway was extended. This stretch of fertile farmland, now dotted with million-dollar estates, golf courses, and affluent restaurants serving the finest products of the region's soil and vines, had been good to his family. Pale, stately egrets, red-tailed hawks, and petite goldfinches were common sights in the South Valley sky. But turkey vultures signaled the presence of death.

"Eufrasio," repeated Fortunato "Lucky" Giardi, snapping his friend out of his daze. "Bartolomeo couldn't get it past the line. It's your toss."

"Oh," Eufrasio said, the noon sun shining from his well-tanned scalp. *"Mi scusi."*

"You still toss like my *nonna*, Baccio," boomed Ottavio "Eight Ball" Tremolada.

Bartolomeo Zanetti's face, creased by sun and time, melted into a cherubic grin. "You hoist bags of manure every day for forty years and see how strong your shoulders are, Ottavio."

Lucky chimed in, "You're just like those bags, Eight Ball. Full of shit."

Eufrasio's knees creaked as he stooped to pick up the *pallina* and sized up the court. He'd heard this puffery before. He sipped the wine in his glass and then gently set it on the table under the sweeping madrone that shaded this end of his backyard.

"Besides," Bartolomeo continued, "my *nonna—Dio riposi la sua anima*," he intoned before making the sign of the cross and kissing the thick gold crucifix that hung from his neck, "could've whipped your *culo grasso* and handed it back to you perfectly seasoned and sautéed for dinner. Watch your mouth."

The two men squared off briefly, then dissolved into hearty laughter and slapped each other on the back. This quartet's friendship spanned nearly half a century. The sons of immigrants, raised in their respective family businesses, had been bonded by the successes and failures of agricultural life here in the Valley of the Heart's Delight. After almost fifty years, nothing could be concealed. They knew all there was to know about each other.

"Secrets run deep like the roots in this valley's fertile soil," Eufrasio had proselytized one night, puffing a cigar as he dealt hands for poker. *"They are protected and passed down from generation to generation. They withstand storms. They spread out and grow in the dark and underground. In places no one can see. But at some point, they always bear fruit."*

"That's why I'm glad we have each other," Lucky said as he assessed his cards.

"Aww, that's nice," Bartolomeo said, dropping a handful of chips into the pot. "I want you all to know I love you like brothers."

Ottavio anted and chimed in, "I feel the same way, *miei amati fratelli*."

Lucky rolled his eyes as his large hand measured out a stack of chips. "You maroons and your mushy talk," he quipped, then tossed his chips into the pile with a sharp clack. "What I meant was, I'm glad we have each other because soon we'll all be so old that we won't remember the stuff we've sworn to keep quiet."

Eufrasio chuckled, sending jagged clouds of acrid smoke into the air. Lucky always found a way to turn a serious moment into something comical. But the underlying sentiment rang true. From working the fields before school and *attending each other's weddings, to the additions of children and then grandchildren, their unofficial fraternity was rooted in shared experiences. Tilled by calloused hands, tended through bumper crops and crippling droughts, nurtured through church festivals, funerals, retirements, and other rites of passage. The foursome, all widowers now, had settled into their roles as elder statesmen, assembling for regular outings. Espresso two afternoons a week. Saturday morning breakfast in town. Dominoes every other Thursday at Miliani's. Their amassed wealth was fractional in comparison to the region's standard of living. But they were happy to give back, attending community fundraisers and charity functions each year to ensure that generations to come would appreciate the rich, bucolic splendor this valley offered.*

Today, that offering included a perfect blue sky, good wine, and a gentle breeze. Eufrasio leaned into the toss, rolling the *pallina* just past the line.

"Ay!" Lucky cheered, slapping Eufrasio's warped hand in a stinging high-five.

Eufrasio stepped back, reached for his glass and let Ottavio take his turn. The stem pinched between his still-tingling fingers, he took in the leathery, fig-infused aroma of his Tempranillo. Life was good, and he was grateful for time with friends and all the fine things decades of hard work had earned him. As he tilted back the bowl, Eufrasio noticed that three more turkey vultures had joined the spiraling flight pattern in the east. With the wine now settling in his mouth, the midday sun reflected from their glossy wings.

Down the slope and across the empty field on the east side of Bel Monte Boulevard, Dion Maggioli's corpse lay prone beneath a lone, majestic oak. No one knew how long he'd been dead, or how he got there. But at twenty-six, Dion—the heir to a garlic-growing dynasty—was bright, energetic, kind-hearted, and well-liked in his community. "High vibration," the millennial *wunderkinds* of Silicon Valley might've called him. A doer. A change agent. An up-and-comer with a head for business and a trust fund to finance any endeavor he could imagine.

But someone had wanted him dead. And here in the revolving shadows of descending vultures, it appeared they had gotten their wish.

| 2 |

Dominic Panicio's phone buzzed from somewhere in his cargo shorts pocket. He swayed in his hammock, the salty Bahamian breeze lulling him back to his post-pina colada nap. Gently crashing waves lapped the shore and Dom let out a pineapple-infused belch, his eyes still closed. When a second buzz from his pocket rousted him, he sat up. He tried to right himself in the hammock with the confidence and grace of a drunken tightrope walker straddling a lava pit. That wasn't just any buzz. Dean Martin crooning "That's Amore" meant the notification could only be from one person: his ex-wife, Florence.

He fumbled a meaty hand through his pocket, causing the hammock to shift. Peering over the side, he saw the pale sand approaching his nose and felt his spine contort.

"Ting-a-ling-a-ling ..." his phone pulsed.

The further he dug in his pocket, the closer he came to the ground. Finally, he pulled out the phone, his stomach twisted in knots, and squinted at the screen.

FOUR DAYS AND NO WORD. WORRIED.

Dom blinked, trying to un-fuzzy the text. Between the pina coladas at lunch and the fact that he'd left his readers in the villa, he could barely focus. But Florence didn't text him often. So, he let another pineapple burp settle and then cartoonishly extricated himself from the hammock, nearly landing on his face. The sand warmed his feet as he hobbled into the villa.

"Hey!" Pauly said, lifting himself from the couch. Or, more specifically, Millie, who was beneath him on the couch. "Can't a couple of newlyweds get some privacy?"

With the glazed tiles cooling his feet, Dom proceeded toward his bedroom. "Suck your faces off, kids. It ain't like I can see nothin' anyway," he called over his shoulder, narrowly missing one of Millie's sisters in the hallway.

"Sorry, Susan."

"It's Marg—" she began. But Dom pushed past the mahogany door jamb and fumbled to his nightstand. Opening the drawer, he retrieved his readers. The frames were too small for his globular head, but he slipped them on, sat on the four-poster bed, and pulled out his phone again. There were more messages now, and it appeared they had arrived out of order.

U GETTING THIS?

FOUR DAYS AND NO WORD. WORRIED.

I NEVER TRUSTED THAT MAN.

CAN U HELP?

DIDI MISSING.

"You all right?" Margaret asked from the doorway.

Dom looked up, his diminutive reading glasses perched on the end of his bulbous nose. "I dunno," he said. "I got these weird texts from Florence. Not sure what they mean."

"Can I see?" Margaret said, stepping into the room. "Susan went to the store. I figured we could give the lovebirds some space."

"Sure," Dom said, handing her the phone as the ceiling fan blades whirred overhead.

"Oh, this isn't good." The rattan chair crackled as she settled into the seat. "Who's Didi? Her sister? A girlfriend?"

Dom removed his readers and raked his fingers through his grey-speckled curls, damp from the sea air. "That's what I'm trying to figure out. Seems like I should know."

Margaret gave the phone back. "Is it possible these messages weren't intended for you?"

Dom shrugged. "Maybe," he began, "but, I got a funny feeling. Something's wrong and because of... the way things were, you know, maybe she's trying to be secretive about it."

"Oh, you mean your years in the 'construction business' and all that?"

Dom pointed at her and winked. "You're a sharp cookie."

Margaret laughed at his clumsy mixed metaphor. "Well, I guess that's better than being dull. You gonna text her back?"

"I feel kinda like a boob—"

Margaret straightened.

"Oh, no offense," Dom said. "I mean, I feel like an idiot for not knowing who she's talking about. And like you said, maybe it wasn't meant for me."

"But no harm in finding out, right?"

Dom nodded and punched a reply into his phone.

YOU OK?

A few minutes went by, and then a solitary Y appeared on his screen.

Then the little dots that indicated Florence was typing bubbled up. Margaret peered over Dom's shoulder, both eagerly awaiting the next reply.

DIDI MISSING CA, it came at last.

"Didi," Dom said, "who the fuck—"

"C-A?" Margaret asked. "Does she mean California?"

"OH, *DIDI*," Dom said, slapping his palm on his forehead. "That's what she calls him."

"Him?"

"Yeah, her nephew," Dom explained. "Except, he ain't really her nephew, *per se.*"

"Oh, I got a few of those," Margaret said. "Nieces, too."

"Yeah, it's complicated, but basically, she was tight with the kid's mom way back in the day, before we got married. Gloria. They went to school together. I never met her, but she and Florence were like two thieves at the hip."

Margaret's head tilted. "You mean, thick as thieves? Joined at the hip?"

"Yeah," Dom said, hastily punching the keypad. It had always been his nature to act first and talk second.

NEED ME TO FIND HIM? WHEN'S THE LAST TIME YOU TALKED TO HIM?

He tapped his fingers on the phone.

"So, tell me about Gloria," Margaret asked as they waited.

"Oh, she did well," Dom said, his eyes glued to the screen. "Married the garlic king."

"The garlic king?"

"Yeah, name's … uh, Mostaciolli. No. Macaroni. Nah, that ain't it. Anyway, she meets this mug on vacation one spring break, right? And he's loaded. Family grows all the garlic distributed in the U.S."

Margaret's eyes widened. "*All* of it?"

"ALL of it," Dom said. "He's full-a cabbage."

"Wait, I thought you said garlic."

"That, too," he said as Margaret shook her head, bewildered. "Anywhoodly-doodly, I ain't ever met these folks. I got the feelin' he didn't want Gloria associatin' with certain types from the old neighborhood, if you get my drift. Even though, from what I heard, he's the same type. Not the family, so much, but he … I dunno. Somethin' about him Flo didn't trust. Gloria was real sad about it but always tried to stay in touch. She would send letters about the kid, maybe some art he made in school, talk about how bright he was. Stuff like that. And every year for Christmas, they sent Flo and me a nice garlic braid, and some giardiniera. The good stuff you set out for Sunday dinner. The best pickled colley-flower—"

"Dom," Margaret urged, trying to rein him in.

"Sorry," he said, "anyway, Gloria was always asking Flo to go out and visit, but—"

ABOUT A WEEK AGO. 23RD MAYBE? SAID HE WAS GOING TO MEET HIS GIRL. TAKE U FOR A DRIVE. HURRY, the incoming text said.

Take you for a drive? Dom wondered what that meant.

I WILL, he typed. WHERE AM I GOING?

After several minutes, there was still no reply.

Margaret looked up from her phone. "Maggioli?"

Dom spun around, "Yeah, ain't that what I said? Maggioli. The garlic king."

She turned her phone so Dom could read the screen. "Looks like we're going to the south end of Santa Clara County. Ooh, and there's a little airport that'll be perfect for my plane. We can fly right in and avoid the big city. They even have a museum full of historical aircraft. Oh, we'll have so much fun!"

"Wait a minute, *we—*"

* * *

Margaret taxied down the runway at the Grovedale airport, the wind at her tail as she pulled into the hangar. As Dom and Pauly helped the ladies out, a breeze rifled through the grass.

"What's that smell?" Margaret asked, noting the pungent wind-borne aroma.

"It smells like—" Susan began.

"Garlic bread," Millie finished.

"Heaven," Dom and Pauly said in unison.

While the men unloaded the bags, Susan inspected the plane. The airport attendant had been kind enough to call them a cab to take them to the nearest car rental office. Then he invited them to tour the museum, set up in three different hangars on the airport's site.

While they browsed the antique aircraft collection, Pauly heard a commotion across the way. He looked through the open door and saw a large young man poking his finger into the chest of the man at the ticket booth.

"Have it ready!" the younger man said. Then he stomped off and jumped into a waiting car, which raised a trail of dust as it pulled out of the dirt lot.

"Ohh," Susan purred, "look at this."

Pauly turned to see a shiny red plane, then stepped closer to hear Susan explain that it was a Globe Swift, a post-World War II two-seater. Her enthusiasm for the vintage aircraft made him forget about the commotion, and he found Millie's hand, pulling her close to him as they walked through the hangars. Half an hour later, they were loaded into a roomy, dark sedan and headed to a house they'd found through a vacation rental site.

"I can't thank you guys enough," Dom said from the front passenger seat. "A few days ago, we were all relaxing in the Bahamas, and now we're here. I appreciate you coming to help me find out what happened to Florence's nephew."

Pauly took one hand off the wheel and clapped it on Dom's shoulder. "That's what we do," he said. "We take care of our own."

"I just don't want to let Flo down, you know? What if I can't find him?"

"We will," Pauly said. "We might be old, but we ain't dumb. Besides, we still got some tricks up our sleeves."

"Keep going down Central Road," Millie said from the backseat. "That rental house is past the train station and then a few blocks."

As they drove, Dom looked out the window, noticing a collection of antique stores, cafés, restaurants, banks, a used bookshop, and even a bowling alley. Four smartly dressed older men in fedoras sat at a table outside one of the cafes, sipping espresso and reading newspapers. Across the street, he saw a large mural featuring huge cloves of garlic. Another mural showed neat rows of grapes and an old biplane resembling Susan's. Even the bicycle racks and utility boxes along this downtown corridor paid homage to its agricultural glory.

"Turn here at the light," Millie directed. "Then look for the pale blue Victorian with the big porch. Should be on the corner."

Pauly spotted it quickly, eased the sedan up the driveway, then shut off the engine. "Okay, ladies and germ, we have arrived."

"I'll open up the house," Susan said, grabbing a leopard print cosmetics bag from the trunk before scooting up the steps. Meanwhile, Pauly handed out smaller pieces of luggage to Margaret and Millie, who then disappeared into the house. Dom hoisted his suitcase from the trunk and turned around, stopping abruptly.

"What?" Pauly asked, turning to look.

Two young ladies waved and smiled at them from the sidewalk. At the end of a narrow, pink leash was a spry Yorkshire terrier, bobbing along as fast as her little legs would take her. She snarled at Dom, who cowered.

"Pixie, be nice!" one of the women said.

Pauly slammed the trunk shut, causing Dom to jump. "What's a matter," he joked, "having a … shocking flashback?" Then he put his hands on his throat and pretended to choke, his tongue lolling to the side before breaking out in laughter.

Dom caught his breath and smacked Pauly upside the head. "Ay, close your head before I conk that big Tuscan melon on your shoulders with a gourd. *Idiota.*"

Pauly gave him a friendly shove then inhaled the fragrant air. "You smell that? Like my nonna's *pasta con cocozza,* heavy on the garlic."

"Reminds me of big family dinners with Eddie," Dom said as they reached the steps.

"God rest his soul," Pauly said.

"Laughing and joking and sharing secrets. Those were the days," Dom recalled, wistful.

"Yeah, but not anymore," Pauly reminded him. "Let's find this kid, huh?"

Dom paused and let Pauly go up the steps ahead of him.

Anything for Florence.

| 3 |

Face down in the fertile Santa Clara Valley soil that had grown his family's fortune was probably not the way Dion Maggioli thought he'd end up, but here he was. The heir to a garlic-growing dynasty, he'd earned an MBA from Stanford, spent time building wells in Africa, volunteered at the local compassion center, and lobbied for better wages and working conditions for immigrant field workers. Though surrounded by wealth, he spent weekends working on his beloved '69 Shelby GT-500, purchased with earnings from an afterschool job at a Greek restaurant. For his morning coffee, he frequented the local roastery, rather than the national chain with eight locations within the city's limits. Besides, they made the best Mexican mocha in town, and supporting small businesses was a personal passion for Dion.

His grandfather, Ignazio, had tapped Dion to take over the garlic enterprise when the time came. That bypassed Dion's father, Carlo, who had been removed from the family business years ago, although Carlo never spoke of it. Dion's mother, Gloria, proudly supported his endeavors, even when others whispered about the way her son had ditched certain traditions and embraced the technology that had raised this valley to an economic superpower.

Smashing his head against the thick, exposed roots of the majestic oak had sealed Dion's fate. Ants filed through his blond curls as buzzards circled above. Now all his wealth and kindness no longer mattered. Once a shining star in the golden coast's lucrative agricultural industry, he'd been discarded like the thin, papery skin that sheathed the savory bulbs grown a few miles from where his corpse would soon be found.

The farmer whose property bordered the land for the feed lot had noticed the vultures circling and landing. Too many to be the usual field mice or mole. He thought it might be a coyote. But instead, he'd found Dion Maggioli, one of this town's most high-profile residents, long deceased, and called the authorities. The Maggioli name carried a lot of weight in this town. So much so that Chief Novak himself came to observe the removal of the corpse.

Not long ago, Dion had sat down with Ignazio to discuss taking over the day-to-day operations of Maggioli Garlic Growers. It would be a long process with many steps, according to Ignazio, stretched over the next few years. Dion patiently listened to his grandfather's plans, stressing the importance of carrying on the family name and upholding their traditions and good standing in the community.

"I understand, Nonno," Dion said from his seat in his grandfather's office that day, "but I think there are ways we can reduce production costs with improved technology. And with more land, we can make our entire operation more sustainable, benefitting the eco-system while still turning a profit. There's a huge parcel available right now. I've had my eye on it and I have some ideas. I've even met with the owner's representative. We could really make an impact on our business and our community with that in our holding."

The old man, shriveled but shrewd, cocked his head when he heard a knock. With a wave of his warped hand, he motioned his wife, Adalgisa, into the room. She wore a chic black pantsuit, her white hair piled into a voluminous updo. With the soft jingle of her gold tennis bracelet, she laid a tray of antipasti and a carafe of sparkling water on the grand walnut desk.

"Grazie," Ignazio said as he clasped her hand and brought it to his lips for a kiss.

"I don't mean to interrupt," she said, smoothing what was left of Ignazio's thinning hair with short, even strokes, "but I thought you might want some refreshments."

"Grazie, Nonna," Dion said, rising to retrieve a pair of crystal old-fashioned glasses from the bar behind him. His grandfather's desk was illuminated by a wall of windows, showcasing a sweeping view of the tranquil valley below. Dion returned with the glasses and proceeded to pour from the carafe.

"Won't you join us?" he asked his grandmother. "I can get another glass."

"No, thank you," Adalgisa said. "I have to meet with the church's decorating committee for the Christmas party at the orphanage."

"In May?" Dion asked, handing his grandfather a glass of water.

"*Good things take time*, mio caro nipote," she explained, laying a hand on his cheek.

He remained standing until she exited the room, then turned back to his grandfather, who was using a frilled toothpick from the center of the tray to pick through the mortadella for the best piece.

"Everybody wants that land. I know the Occhipintis have been trying to acquire it for their vineyards," Ignazio said without looking up, his glassy, hazel eyes focused on the tray.

"But they can't offer what I can offer," Dion replied.

His frail hand quivering, Ignazio speared the mortadella he'd targeted. "That's a deal you don't want to be a part of, believe me. Shady characters. Chi va con lo zoppo, impara a zoppicare. Besides, that land's no good for garlic. Too much clay."

"Who said I wanted to grow garlic?"

Leaning toward the slice of mortadella inches from his open mouth, Ignazio abruptly sat up straight, sunbeams spilling in from the windows and illuminating his shoulders like a mandorla. "Oh?"

***

"Daddy, I know what I'm doing," Chavonne Occhipinti cooed into her gold iPhone the same day. With French-manicured nails, she tapped the key card against the door of her midnight silver metallic Model S and swung into the driver's seat. Placing a black peep-toed Louboutin on the brake, she put the car in gear, then set her phone in the bejeweled car mount. "Yes, I've looked into it. More than enough acreage. And I can get us a good price."

Though they'd kept their romance quiet, she was convinced Dion would gift her that parcel for their wedding. It was better suited to growing grapes than garlic, and he knew how much she wanted it. Her family demanded loyalty, and if he planned to marry her, he'd be smart to make such a grand gesture.

Her chestnut hair swished as she looked over her shoulder and pulled out of her parking space at Vista Verde, a golf course with a high-end spa and restaurant. A quick glance at the time indicated she'd be late for her lunch date with Dion. She checked her makeup in the rearview mirror, brown eyes perfectly lined, lips pouty and red. But her father was still questioning her expertise in this financial matter, wondering if her brothers were better qualified to close the deal.

"Nunzio and Silvestro can't make it happen," she said, trying to harness the irritation in her voice, "not with their outdated ways of doing business. Daddy, I told you, I know what I'm doing. But I'm late for an appointment. Just let me handle it, okay? All right, love you."

Chavonne hung up and purred down the hill on Collina Avenue. She passed the three abandoned outbuildings then waited at the stop sign. Once an old truck with a load of tomatoes went by, she pulled onto Bel Monte Boulevard. Not wanting to delay her lunch date, her Tesla roared around the tomato truck, parallel to the feed lot, then cut back into the southbound lane to avoid a honking Prius. As she pulled parallel with the lone oak, she saw the light at Kennedy was turning from yellow to red.

OMW, she tapped into her phone as she breezed through the intersection.

When her phone rang, she answered without checking the Caller ID, expecting Dion.

"Sorry, sweetie, I'm running late," she said, navigating around a cyclist.

"Sweetie?" the caller said. "That's a new tone, Ms. Occhipinti. Not that I mind."

"Oh, I didn't realize it was you," she explained. "Sorry."

With a sigh of impatience, the voice said, "We need to talk about this land deal."

| 4 |

Kate Kendall peered out her third story window at the corner of Central Road and Oakhurst Street. It was the perfect spot for a newspaper reporter's apartment. Steps away from most of the city's influential businesses and the train station, it was situated above one of the best restaurants in town, Miliani's. Originally established as a hotel in the early 1920s, the Mission-style building was a whistle stop on the route to Los Angeles and oozed with character. From Art Deco décor to a vintage horseshoe bar, it harkened back to a different era. Clark Gable and Will Rogers had been noted visitors. Rumors persisted of mysterious tunnels and brothels connected to the building. Not to mention ghosts. But for Kate, it was the welcoming aroma of the nightly family lasagna dinner that sealed the deal when she visited to inquire about renting. She was barely through the door of the tiny studio apartment when she told the manager she'd take it.

She watched the traffic roll by, then glanced across the street to an eatery now occupying the old city hall space. Peaches leapt to her perch in the bay window, swishing her tail against Kate's arm before settling on the needlepoint pillow. The orange tabby kneaded her paws into the cushion as Kate petted her head. Four men in fedoras shuffled down the sidewalk.

"Peaches," Kate said, as it was her habit to talk out ideas with her cat, "remind me to look into those guys one of these days."

The cat flicked her tail and purred, content with her respite in the morning sun.

"But today," Kate felt obligated to explain on the way to her desk, "I'm looking into someone else. I want to know why Carlo Maggioli isn't part of his family's business anymore."

As Peaches' soft snores drifted through the cramped studio, Kate's booted up her laptop. She sipped from her *Town Crier* work swag mug. Already cold. She really had to get better about watching the time. She took a second sip, then got up to put the mug in the microwave.

Worse.

After dumping it down the sink, she went back to her desk and tapped into the city's vital records database. She knew the drill. There were tons of entries, given that the family had been here for multiple generations and owned a considerable amount of land. Sifting through them was a chore. She checked the notes on her pad.

"Left off page 13."

She typed into the search bar.

MAGGIOLI, CARLO

But before she could skip to the bottom of the page, something new caught her eye.

Death Certificate. Dion Maggioli. Son of CARLO MAGGIOLI and Gloria Maggioli.

Dated just a few days ago.

"Death Certificate?"

※ ※ ※

"Thank you all for being here," Ignazio Maggioli announced to the somber group assembled in his office. Adalgisa stood behind him, her hand on his shoulder. "I know I speak for all of us when I say I am devastated at the loss of Dion. Such a promising future, and now his bright spark has been extinguished. Just two months ago, he was here in my office, and we talked about how to make the transition for him to take over Maggioli Garlic Growers."

Sullen faces stared back at him. There was Gloria, Dion's mother, draped in a long black dress, dark hair pulled into a low ponytail. Her eyes puffed and moist from tears. A tissue folded into her petite hand. Next to her was Carlo. His gray suit jacket hung loosely on his thin frame, skimming the hips of his dark jeans. His white shirt collar open and a thick gold chain at his neck. Since being asked to leave the board and relinquish his position in the company several years ago, Carlo hadn't felt the need to wear a proper suit and tie. His salt and pepper hair, slicked back on the sides, fell in loose, straggly waves at his shoulders. Behind them were Ignazio's older sisters, Ysabella and Lucrezia, and their younger brother, Tomasso. Two of Maggioli's most esteemed board members, Vincenzo Ferreira and Hugo Cardenas, sat nearby. There was a pecking order here, an unspoken rule about being part of a family business without being part of the family. Enzo and Hugo had both worked the land in the early days when Ignazio was still purchasing plots and tilling his own soil. Over time, they had ingratiated themselves to their friend and founder, but there was still an invisible line there. One that those who didn't share the same blood knew they could never cross.

"Now," Ignazio continued, "though it appears to be an accident, I know the police are investigating. I've asked Chief Novak to use the utmost discretion in handling Dion's case. As far as I know, there's been no coverage. What we don't need is negative media attention."

Carlo shifted in his seat. Gloria's damp eyes focused on the view of the valley as her hand found Carlo's.

"Jake has always been a friend to the Maggiolis," Ignazio said, "and if this was not an accident, I hope with his oversight we can expect a timely arrest without every detail of our business being dragged through the news."

"Are there any leads?" Lucrezia asked from behind her short black veil.

"I don't understand what he was doing there," Tomasso said.

"Who would want to harm Didi?" Ysabella chimed in, as if anyone had a legitimate answer. Gloria bit her lip and sobbed quietly into the handkerchief Carlo had offered her.

"No leads yet," Ignazio said. "No one knows why he was there. And I can't imagine why anyone would do this."

Adalgisa patted his shoulder again, then began to rub his back as sobs filled the room.

"It's so unfair," Hugo said. "I want to extend our condolences, on behalf of myself, Maria, and our entire family. Dion was such a kind soul. We will miss him deeply."

"And please," Enzo spoke up, "let us know if there's anything we can do. I know this is a difficult time. Hugo and I will be happy to help in any way we can."

"Thank you, I appreciate that," Ignazio said. "The two of you are almost like family to us. I think the next order of business is to plan a funeral. Gloria?"

She straightened herself and exhaled. "It's only been two days since he was found," she said. "We've not really had time to think about …" She trailed off, her tears flowing again.

"Papa," Carlo said, "we want to honor Dion, but I don't know how we can do that and still keep things quiet. He deserves a big tribute. We could fill Sainte Cecelia's twice over with all the people he touched, all who benefitted from his kindness. How do we celebrate his life without drawing attention to his death?"

The phone on Ignazio's desk buzzed. "There's a delivery for you," his secretary, Patty, said over the speaker. "I'm sorry to interrupt, but there's nowhere else to put this."

Enzo went to the door. When he opened it, he was met with a giant floral wreath perched on an easel. He helped Patty steer it into the room. Orange gladioli sprays entwined with white roses and lilies scenting the air. A cream ribbon trailed downward, embroidered with a message.

"With our sincerest condolences, The Occhipinti Family."

"How very kind of Lazaro and Rialta to send that," Ignazio said. "Patty, please be sure to send them a thank you note before you leave tonight."

"Yes sir," she replied before scooting out of the room.

Once the door was closed, Ignazio tented his hands and held them to his chin. "I see the effort to keep this quiet is going to be a challenge. I don't understand how the Occhipintis knew about this when we've been so careful."

"Bad news travels fast," Tomasso said. "It won't be long before everyone knows."

"Well," Gloria said, standing and limping over to look at the enormous arrangement. She leaned toward the lilies, taking a sniff, "Dion was friendly with Chavonne Occhipinti."

"Friendly?" Carlo questioned, almost chuckling. "If that's what you want to call it."

"Oh?" Adalgisa said. "I never knew they were friends. What's this?"

"Much more than friends, Mama," Carlo said. "They kept it quiet, but you might as well know. Dion and Chavonne had been dating for a while. I think they were getting serious."

Ignazio sank back in his chair. "I had no idea," he said. "Why didn't you tell me?"

"Because it wasn't my business," Carlo said. "Not that you give a damn about that."

"Carlo—" Adalgisa began.

Ignazio raised his hand, signaling concession. "I know you're upset," he said. "But this isn't the time for old grievances. We're here for Dion. Everything else can wait for another day."

Enzo and Hugo exchanged a glance as Carlo puffed out his cheeks.

"You're right," Carlo finally said. "But you know, I wouldn't be all that surprised if the Occhipintis had something to do with this."

"Carlo!" Adalgisa exclaimed. "That's quite an accusation."

"Son," Ignazio said, leaning forward, "I have known the Occhipintis as long as I've lived in this valley. Lazaro has a keen sense for business that can sometimes lean toward ruthlessness. I've seen him make some questionable deals and turn his head from unethical practices. But I wouldn't consider him, or anyone in his family, capable of murder."

Carlo slapped a hand on Ignazio's desk, causing Adalgisa and Gloria to jump. "His sons and their associates are little more than common thugs—"

"And I will not stand for you making such accusations without evidence," Ignazio calmly countered, his filmy hazel eyes fixed on Carlo.

The father and son exchanged a long, uncomfortable glare before Carlo stood.

"Come on, Gloria," he said. "We have a funeral to plan."

"But Carlo," she said, an apologetic expression on her face as he grabbed her hand.

"Now," he said, his hand on her back. She struggled to keep up with him as he escorted her to the door.

"Carlo—" Adalgisa began again.

"Let him go," Ignazio said, waving him off. "He needs time to cool down."

As Carlo slammed the door, the room silenced. Ignazio focused on the door briefly, then turned to the group.

"Do you think this will bring to light Carlo's … transgressions?" Tomasso asked, his voice weak and thin.

Enzo and Hugo shared another glance, knowing better than to interfere in family business.

"What would it matter if it did?" Lucrezia said, her veil fluttering as she exhaled in disgust and sat back in her chair. "Nothing will bring Didi back."

"I'll say what we're all thinking. Carlo is the reason we're in this mess," Tomasso replied. "Those loans are coming due soon. And the land deal Dion was working on would've solved our financial problems. I can't help but wonder if Dion's death might be connected to…"

As Ysabella sobbed softly, Enzo leaned over to offer her a crisp white handkerchief.

Ignazio shook his head, his brow furrowed. "Well, one thing I do know," he finally said, "is that while the authorities investigate Dion's death, there's a good chance they'll want to look at our company's finances. And that is unwelcome attention right now. We all know the past few years have been … difficult. And how much we've strived to keep our financial struggles quiet. I'm afraid we may not be able to protect our secrets much longer. But, as I said before, I'm hopeful that Chief Novak will be a man of his word and extend us the courtesy of discretion."

Enzo and Hugo looked at each other once more as Ysabella let out a mournful wail. Adalgisa patted Ignazio's shoulder and the patriarch stared out the window, taking in the moody shadows on the valley's dappled hills.

* * *

Days later, as the pipe organ echoed the final tones of the dirge, Kate Kendall's sensible heels clacked on the stone floor of Sainte Cecelia's. "Mr. Maggioli! Carlo!" she called, hurrying to catch up to the family members before they disappeared into the identical black sedans lining the curb. Carlo's long, silvered hair ruffled in the breeze as he turned toward her.

"Mr. Maggioli," she said, nearly breathless and reaching into her purse for a small electronic device, "I'm sorry for your loss. My name's Kate Kendall. Can I get a statement for the *Town Crier?*"

Carlo held the door open for Gloria, shaking his head.

"Mr. Maggioli," Kate continued, holding the recorder in her hand, "I'd like to get a statement from the family. Why is Dion's death being kept quiet?"

Carlo spun around, his dark sunglasses barely containing his glare. "How dare you ask such a thing? This is a private family matter. You're not welcome here."

She stood firm. "Dion was only twenty-six. Did he have health issues?"

"It's none of your business," Carlo managed, his face growing red.

"Was he murdered?"

Without warning, Carlo swatted the recorder from her hand, sending it crashing to the sidewalk. The blow dislodged the batteries and they rolled into the street. He lifted his foot, poised to stomp on the device. But before he could complete this act of rage, Ignazio stepped in.

"Carlo, *basta!* That's enough," he said. The younger Maggioli shrugged, straightened his jacket, then climbed into the back of the sedan and slammed the door. Ignazio turned to Kate, "Our family will have no comment at this time, Miss Kendall. I request that you respect our privacy. Please send my office an invoice for a new recorder, plus a day's wages. I'll double it and have it paid immediately. Now, if you will excuse me, I have a grandson to mourn."

Ignazio walked to the sedan ahead of Carlo's, leaving Kate on the sidewalk. She pushed her strawberry blonde hair behind her ear and crouched to gather her recorder as the sedans left.

"I bet there's my answer," she said.

| 5 |

Dom paused to let a quartet of well-dressed, elderly men clear the crosswalk. One smiled and tipped his fedora. Pauly waved to the man as Dom accelerated, passing the city's cluster of retail outlets. Within ten minutes, Dom was cruising the country road east of the freeway. Surrounded by lush gold foothills that gently ebbed into verdant pastures, the two-lane road was rife with potholes. The rented sedan jostled them as Pauly studied a map on his phone.

"Says the place is on the left, about eight more miles," he advised.

"Nice and quiet out here," Dom said, noting the signs for various ranches, stables, and cellars. "So, tell me again how we found these people?"

"Millie and Susan looked up Florence's friend, Gloria," Pauly began. "Her son Dion—DiDi, Florence calls him—is involved in the family business. Looks like he's a good kid. In fact, he was named as one of Silicon Valley's most eligible bachelors last year."

"Good for him. Bet that guy gets lots of chicks."

"Probably. Graduated from Stanford. Involved with charities and non-profits. Clean water, environmental causes, feeding the homeless, stuff like that. Works with his grandfather."

"Not his father? Family business, right?"

"Now that's interesting," Pauly said. "They looked up the whole family, and Dion's father, Carlo, is barely mentioned anywhere."

Dom slowed for a stop sign and let a propane truck pass before proceeding through the intersection. "Weird. Thought he was the garlic king?"

"Yeah, he used to be vice president," Pauly continued. "Or something like that."

"Like an underboss?"

"Right. Clearly, poised to take over when his old man, Ignazio, was gone. And then, for some reason, he dropped out of sight."

"Like disappeared? I wonder if Flo knows that."

"No, he's still around. He's just not involved in the company. Isn't even on the board."

"How bad you gotta fuck up to get kicked outta your family's company?" Dom mused.

"Yeah, the girls were wondering that, too," Pauly said. "So, they did more digging. Turns out the Maggiolis aren't the only wealthy family with questionable history in this area."

Dom watched a crow descend into a rambling vineyard. "Every family has secrets."

"Yeah, well get this. The Maggiolis grow garlic, right? And they own a lot of land."

"So?"

"So, this land ain't cheap. And they've owned it for generations; bought it back when it wasn't so expensive. They just happened to get here first. But they're always trying to buy up neighboring parcels of land to expand their enterprise. There's just one problem."

"And what's that?"

"This whole area was settled by immigrants who worked the land," Pauly said, "and there are a few of these family 'dynasties,' if you will, in the area. All built on agriculture. All incredibly wealthy, thanks to the good fortune of being in the right place at the right time, so they could build a business for future generations. And... they all *hate* each other."

"Really?"

"Yeah, lotta bad blood. They play nice at public functions, participate in city council activities, and do their civic duties. But they've drug each other to court and accused each other of questionable business practices for decades."

"An old school turf war," Dom chuckled. "Right up our dark and shady alley, huh?"

"Exactly," Pauly said. "And the older generation is aging to a point where they'll need their heirs to take over and keep the businesses going. Probably evolve with the times, you know? But none of them want to sell to the others. So that drives up the price."

"Which means that practically no one can afford it—"

"Except another one of these families," Pauly finished. "Or, outside investors, which is extremely frowned upon. People here want to keep things local."

"I see," Dom said, slowing down. "What did you say the address was?"

Pauly checked his phone. "12165, up here on the left."

Dom pulled into a driveway, stopping at the wrought iron gate with an interlocking M C.

"Hello?" crackled the deep voice from an intercom nestled into a brick pillar.

"Hello," Dom said. "We're here to see ..." he fumbled in his pocket for a piece of paper and squinted at Pauly's handwriting, "uh, Miguel da ... da ... oh, help me out here."

"Da Conceicao," came the voice with a soft chuckle.

"Duh cone-say-soh," Dom repeated. "Yeah, Miguel da ... what you said."

The wrought iron scraped the black asphalt as the gate slowly swung open.

"Come up to the house and park by the cherry orchard," the voice instructed.

Dom pulled through the gates and ascended the lengthy black path, his eyes flitting toward water fountains and religious statuary on either side. It was a gentle grade, offset by clusters of sunny daffodils, bearded irises in calm shades of cream and lavender, and tall, cheerful pink rose bushes. A lush green lawn dramatically set off the flowers. But the entire tableau was just an accent to the property's most stunning feature: an enormous, white Greek revival farmhouse. A dozen limestone steps plateaued into a wide, Doric-columned porch, with a twin balcony resting above. A cupola emerged from the black slate roof, centered between two stone chimneys and a bank of shallow windows.

"Madonn'," Dom said, "this is some place. Tell me what we know about these people."

Pauly hunched to look toward the rows of stone fruit trees. "Miguel and Mathilde da Con … yeah, whatever. Anyway, they owned an orchard next to Occhipinti Vineyards."

"Occhipinti? Sicilian, yeah?"

"Yeah," Pauly echoed.

"Means," Dom said, steering the car toward the blossoming cherry trees, "painted eyes."

"Correct," Pauly agreed.

"But these folks, the De Con-whatchamacallits, they're not Sicilian?"

"Portuguese," Pauly said.

"De Conceicao is Portuguese?"

"*Da* Conceicao."

"Duh?"

"Duh."

Dom cocked his head.

"D-A, Da," Pauly explained. "Susan learned they made a fortune growing cherries, peaches, nectarines, plums, and the like. I think the grandfather or great-grandfather settled here originally. But they don't own the orchard anymore."

Dom eased the car into a marked space, shaded by an overhang of cherry branches. "The birds are gonna shit all over this," he observed. "So why don't they own the orchard anymore?"

"Are you familiar with Silicon Valley real estate values?"

"This is Silicon Valley? Where they do computer parts? Self-driving cars? Tech bros?"

"The south end of it," Pauly said. "They call it South County. Anyway, Miguel had an arrangement with the Occhipintis. Sold his land so he could retire. Must have made bank, too."

Dom glanced at the house, glistening in the midday sun like it had sprung from the pages of a glossy architectural magazine. *"Niente merda,"* he said, shutting off the car.

A large man in a long-sleeved shirt, dark Wranglers, and a sun hat approached from the house's side porch. He waved as Dom and Pauly exited the car and within four strides, he stood before them, extending a beefy hand.

"Welcome," he said, "I'm Miguel da Conceicao."

Dom shook his hand, knees weakening at the man's grip. "Dom Pan—uh, Dominic *Ponte*. Nice to meet you. And this is my friend, Pauly *Messina*."

"A pleasure to meet you," Miguel said, dwarfing Pauly's hand with his crippling grasp. "Please, come in. Mathilde has just made some lemonade for us."

He led them up the steps, removed his boots, and ushered them into the stately home. Weathered iron sconces and large stone urns flanked either side of the tremendous black door, inset with leaded glass. The parlor featured a massive glass chandelier, gracefully hovering from an intricately carved plaster medallion. A bucolic mural of blossoming trees stretched up the staircase wall, set off by forged iron railings. Above the entry table was a large, yellowing photograph. Protected by thick, blue-tinted glass was a thin man in a thin suit. In his slender fingers, he held a wide-brimmed Panama-style hat, similar to the one Miguel had just placed on a rack by the front door. His face, furrowed by sun exposure, was gentle but tough all at once. Undoubtedly, the face of an immigrant. Dom's family had a gallery of similar photos in their cozy Staten Island cottage. Each a tribute to an unrelenting dream of a better life elsewhere.

"My *bisavo*," Miguel said. "Joaozinho Filomen da Conceicao. He sailed here from Portugal in the late 1800s."

Dom and Pauly nodded as they took it all in. "*Bisavo?* Your grandfather?"

Miguel shook his head, "Great grandfather."

"Good afternoon," said a soft voice. The woman wore a simple cotton dress and carried a round platter. On it was a pitcher of pale lemonade, dotted with fresh lemon slices and ice cubes, and four tall glasses. "I'm Mathilde. Won't you come this way?"

They followed her to a gathering table in the next room, laid with several small plates. There were chunks of linguica, a wheel of soft cheese, a small bowl of green olive dip, marinated red pepper strips, and sliced, crusty bread.

Dom looked at the mix of grand, Old World charm and homey, comfortable furnishings. "You have a lovely home," he said. "Thank you for welcoming us. I hope we're not intruding."

"We're glad to have you," Miguel said, standing until Mathilde was seated, then pushing in her chair. "Tell me, what brings you to South County?"

Dom exhaled. "I'm afraid it's not a happy occasion," he said. "I'm trying to track down a young man, a friend of a friend. And my friend is concerned because she hasn't heard from him."

Miguel sipped his lemonade and set down the glass. "What's this young man's name?"

Dom pursed his lips, knowing that once he uttered the name, he was opening them up to all sorts of potential scenarios. "Dion," he finally said. "Dion Maggioli."

Miguel's brow twitched, while the rest of his face remained motionless. His large hand rested next to his lemonade glass. Dom's stomach clenched, wondering if he'd made a mistake.

"Dion," Miguel said, "a fine, generous young man."

Dom felt his stomach relax, enough to spear a piece of linguica and bite into it. Strongly flavored with paprika and garlic, it had a dryness he didn't expect. A swig of his lemonade washed it down and he pushed down a burp, tucking his chin into his neck.

"And have you seen him recently?" Dom asked.

Miguel sat back in his chair. "Been a while. He comes by about once a month."

"To do business?" Pauly asked.

"No," Miguel laughed, "just to chat. He's a nice kid. Smart, too. Has some great ideas about the future of agriculture. I mean, it never *feels* like business."

"What do you mean by that?" Dom said.

"I mean, I think Dion comes by to pick my brain," Miguel said, "so maybe it is business, but I don't think of it like that. In some ways, I think I'm like a father figure to him. Don't get me wrong. It's not that he and Carlo aren't close. I think they are. But Carlo, well … he's not really known for making the best decisions. And Dion and I talk about all sorts of things. Life, you know. Relationships. How to make the world a better place. And, of course, agriculture. He'll say, 'Big Mike, what's the secret to tending alluvial soil?' So, I try to help."

"Alluvial?" Dom questioned.

"The soil we have here in this part of the valley," Miguel explained. "Alluvial means it's been eroded by water and redeposited elsewhere. You find it near floodplains, rivers, deltas. All over California, but especially rich here."

"And it's good for orchards?" Pauly asked while Mathilde refilled his glass.

"It can be," Miguel said, holding his glass out for Mathilde. "Orchards do best in mountainous soil. But the earth here is so full of minerals, thanks to the sediment of the alluvial soil, that we've been quite fortunate."

"What about garlic?" Dom asked.

"It's funny," Miguel said, "garlic grows best in a sandy loam. The soil must be loose, and you need to make sure it drains well. There's a whole science to it. How much clay, proper pH, all that. But garlic has done very well here, as I'm sure you're aware. Otherwise, you wouldn't be asking about Dion Maggioli. You must know his family's business."

Dom nodded. "So, what about grapes? We saw a lot of signs for wineries and tasting rooms when we drove out here. I thought the wine country was up north, in Napa Valley?"

After a long sip of his lemonade, Miguel said, "Wine is one of this region's best, most profitable industries. And the soil is extraordinary.

Now, you need to be somewhat of a chemist to figure it out. But South County has some of the best soil for grapes in the U.S. and the climate is similar to the Mediterranean. Immigrants came here during the Gold Rush and started planting grapes. The soil has a comparable richness to that of Sicily."

"Without the volcano," Dom quipped.

Miguel let out a hearty laugh. "Thank goodness. But the ash from Mt. Etna is what gives Sicilian soil the high mineral content which allows their wine industry to thrive. In fact, one of the largest wine growers here is a family who originally emigrated from Sicily. The Occhipintis."

"And do you know them?" Pauly asked.

"Oh, heavens yes," Miguel sighed. "Forever. You can't live in this valley without knowing the Occhipintis, or at least feeling their influence. I sold them some land, in fact, so I could retire. You see, it's just Mathilde and me. We never had children."

Dom noticed Mathilde's eyes dart to her lap as her husband spoke. Miguel placed his hand over hers and gave it a gentle squeeze.

"Anyway," he resumed, "with no one to take over the business, I realized I could sell and make a nice enough profit to stay here and live very comfortably. So, when Lazaro Occhipinti approached me—well, actually, he sent one of his associates, a kid named D'Agostini—"

He turned to his wife, "That reminds me, I saw him at the feed lot a couple weeks ago, buying boots. He told me to say hello to you. Seemed like he was in a hurry when I tried to chat with him. It was taking them a while to find him a size 12 and said he had to get to a job."

Big Mike turned back to his guests. "Sorry. Sometimes my mind gets a little sidetracked. Come to think of it, when I was leaving, I saw Dion, too. Well, sort of. I saw his Mustang go down the road. But I haven't seen him since then. Anyway," Miguel continued, "selling wasn't a difficult decision. The Occhipintis' property backed up to mine. Laz was very interested in acquiring it. Said it would help his family do more for the valley."

"Do more?" Dom tried.

Miguel let out another laugh. "Oh, I'm no fool. I knew he was only thinking about the bottom line, not giving back to the community. The Occhipintis don't get involved in anything if it's not going to benefit them, somehow."

Dom spread some olive dip on a piece of bread. "I guess there's a lot of folks like that."

"But Dion's not one of them," Mathilde said. "In fact, I know he's considering purchasing a large parcel of land northwest of here. With his own money."

"To expand the family business?" Pauly asked.

"I don't think so," Mathilde replied. "I know he and Miguel talked about it, but I don't think he's ever said. Anyway, I don't think it's for the garlic business."

"Right. I didn't get that impression," Miguel said. "That land isn't really suited for growing garlic. Too sandy, I think. So, tell me, Dominic—"

"Dom, please."

"Dom, you said your friend hasn't heard from Dion and is concerned about him. I can't imagine him running into any kind of trouble. He's a bright young man, kind heart, and from what I've seen, a wonderful future ahead of him."

"Oh, taking over the family business? Sure," Pauly jumped in.

Miguel smiled. "Well, yes, but—and maybe I'm out of line for saying this, because I don't think either family knows yet—but he told me he's planning to get engaged soon."

"Really?" Dom said, surprised. "Who's the lucky lady?"

Miguel turned to Mathilde and smiled. "Chavonne Occhipinti."

After some hearty handshakes and a promise to visit Big Mike and Mathilde any time they were in the area, Dom and Pauly were back on the road.

"You're quiet," Pauly said after a couple miles of silence on the long country road.

"Maybe I don't know how it works here in sunny California," Dom began, "but where we're from, in our, uh, *former business,* you don't go around picking forbidden fruit. You know? Dion sounds like a great kid, but what's he doing with this Occhipinti chick as his *comare*?"

"Yeah, that seemed odd to me, too," Pauly said.

"And," Dom continued, "what's with the land deal? Why would he use his own money to buy land that isn't suited growing his family's crop?"

"But, perfectly suited for growing his soon-to-be fiancée's family's grapes?"

"Ba-da-boom," Dom said, slapping the steering wheel. "And what's with his dad? Flo said Gloria got distant after she started dating him, like he's the reason they didn't keep in touch. I wanna know more about that guy."

"Speaking of Florence," Pauly said, "have you been able to reach her?"

"I texted her when we got here, and again last night to let her know we were going to check things out. She hasn't gotten back to me yet, but my phone shows the messages as read." After a brief silence, Dom continued, "I just don't want to let her down. Done enough of that."

Pauly looked at Dom. "I told you before," he said, "you won't. Don't worry about it."

Dom braked for a stop sign. He blinked hard, suddenly overcome with emotion. "I hadn't thought about it before she texted me," he said, clearing his throat, "but I didn't realize how important it is for me to make things right with her."

"Dom," Pauly said, his voice low, "she's remarried now. You remember that, right?"

Dom sniffed. "I know, I know," he said before letting out a nervous chuckle. "Lookit me. After all these years. *E stupido.*"

Past the majestic estate of the da Conceicaos, the landscape gave way to more humble structures. Fading cottages with worn siding, paled by years in the beating sun. A slim creek trickled along the rutted road, stray poppies shooting up now and then. They came upon a field packed with workers bent from the waist, cultivating plants in long, deep rows. Their only shade was a large billboard, set off with electric lights.

VISIT OCCHINPINTI CELLARS

South County's Premier Winery, Upholding the Traditions of the Old Country

Tasting room open daily, noon to 5 p.m.

The billboard featured a collage of luscious, dew-kissed grapes on the vine, a sweeping estate twice the size of the one they'd just left, assorted wine bottles, and a photogenic family with deep tans, coordinated outfits, and bright, white smiles, posed amid tawny oak barrels.

"Wow," Pauly managed, his mouth falling open at the sight of the young brown-haired woman near the center of the family portrait. "That's some good-lookin' group. I can see why Gloria's nephew might be dizzy with that dame and want a piece of her family's action."

"Those young guys, though," Dom said, noting the muscular, tight-shirted fellas on either side of the woman he presumed was Chavonne.

"Like looking at our own past," Pauly noted.

"Madonn', you ain't kiddin'," Dom said, jarred by the resemblance. "Lookin' like a coupl'a droppers waitin' to get made."

"Absolutely."

The sedan inflated with a suffocating silence as they drove. Finally, Dom said, "I don't miss that life."

Pauly shook his head. "Me neither. I don't think I could ever go back."

"Ever?"

"Ever."

But as they drove, Dom's mind wandered to the old days. Stacks of Mazuma at his disposal. Staying ready to put the screws on some peacher, pump him full of metal if needed, collect juice when it was due. Trying his best to keep outta the nippers, no matter what. It was an addiction. And like most addictions, a destructive one. But why did it have to be so ... addictive?

Pauly broke the silence, "Maybe the girls might wanna go wine tasting someday?"

Dom turned to him and smiled. "I like the way you think, *paisan*."

| 6 |

Chavonne placed the petals on a blank page her journal. The bouquet was the last gift Dion had given her—sweet pink and cream roses, sent "just because"—and she wanted to preserve them. She knew his family wouldn't want her at his funeral. And the last thing she wanted to do was cause a scene. Other than visiting his crypt at the cemetery one day when she could slip in unnoticed, this would be her last memory of him. The only way to have him with her. She closed the journal's brown leather cover and pressed it tight.

Theirs had been a whirlwind courtship. Her family had discouraged them from interacting, though they often attended the same events. "They don't do business like we do," her father had warned, leaving the obvious unsaid. "They look out for their interests. We look out for our interests. You don't want to mix with that crowd, Princess." But after years of noticing each other at chamber of commerce luncheons, city council meetings, and charity fundraisers, it was Dion who struck up a conversation in the most unsuspecting place: outside Starbucks.

She was on her way to her car, parked in the red zone while she'd gone to pick up her drink. He was crouched at the driver's window of a burgundy Oldsmobile from the 1970s, chatting with a man in tattered clothes and offering part of a breakfast sandwich to the man's scruffy dog. Chavonne had frowned when she saw him. When she'd parked, she blocked the path of the Olds. Seemed like that guy parked here, in the same spot, regularly. Likely living out of his car. The city ordinance said he only had to move it once a day. She'd seen him take it around the parking lot and pull back into the same space. He usually said good morning to her. Sometimes the dog yapped. Other times it snarled. But she never paid him much attention. She was here to get her caffeine fix and be on her way. Being the chief business development officer of Occhipinti Enterprises meant she didn't have time to chit chat with the unhoused.

"Hey," Dion said, standing up as she breezed by. "My friend Walter here is wondering when you might move your vehicle. He needs to get to an appointment."

She waved her cup of skinny hazelnut mocha in their direction and unlocked the door.

An appointment, my ass. With whom? A bottle of rum?

"Hey," he repeated, "Miss Occhipinti."

She turned and glared at him, displeased at the way he'd used her name here in public, especially following such a common interjection like "hey." The guy living in the Oldsmobile didn't need to know who she was.

"Yes," she said, one raspberry wool trousered-leg already inside the car. "What?"

"This is a red zone, Miss Occhipinti," Dion said. "It's illegal to park here."

"So? This store doesn't have a drive-thru. And I was only a few minutes. Would've been out sooner if they'd gotten my order right."

Dion frowned. "But you blocked Walter's car."

"And now I'm going," she eased into the car and lowered the window, "Mr. Maggioli."

Two could play this game.

She cleared the end of the Oldsmobile and was starting to pull away when he stepped in front of her, holding up his hand. She slammed on the brakes, causing her coffee to spill.

"Are you crazy? I could've hit you! And now look what you've done," she said, grabbing a microfiber cloth from the console to dab at the coffee splattered over her dash.

"You owe Walter an apology," he said calmly, his eyes pleading.

It was those eyes that drew her in. Mellow like macchiato and slightly droopy at the outer edges, lined with long, lush lashes. Kind and gentle, yet full of authority. Thick, curly blond hair, streaked by the sun, grazed his shoulders. A hunter green shirt, tucked into dark jeans and cuffed at the wrist, stretched over his muscular frame. And then he smiled. A warm, soft grin lifting the corners of his full lips. Chavonne stared at him, oblivious to the hot coffee seeping into her air vent, captivated by this charismatic man who had the nerve to call out her bad behavior.

"Well?" he said, waiting.

"You're right," she finally said. With a freshly manicured nail in the shade to match her suit, she lowered the passenger window and leaned forward. "Walter," she called to the man. He was petting the dog, a wet nose nuzzled to his grimy cheek. When she called his name, he turned, revealing his long, greasy, black hair and wiry beard. "Walter, I'm sorry."

His face dissolved into a semi-toothless smile as he waved back.

Dion had walked over to the passenger window and reached inside her low-profile sports car. "Sorry about your drink," he said, wiping the cup with a handkerchief monogrammed with a dark blue M. "You off to work?"

"Yeah," she said, watching him sop up the liquid from the dashboard, careful to avoid pushing it into the vent. "You don't have to do that."

"No trouble," he said, extending a hand. "We've never really been introduced. I'm Dion."

"I know who you are," she said, tucking her petite hand inside his. "Chavonne."

He smiled that warm grin again and squeezed her hand. "I know who you are."

A honk came from behind her as Walter backed out and waved from the Oldsmobile before lumbering out into the main path of the parking lot. Dion waved back.

"I need to go," Chavonne said. "I'm supposed to be leading a meeting in ten minutes."

Dion backed away, holding his damp handkerchief. He folded it and started to tuck it in his pocket, then thought better of it. "Enjoy the rest of your day, Chavonne," he said with a wink.

Unsure of how to respond, she waved goodbye and rolled up the window. The drive to the office went quickly. She was still late, but it felt like time had stopped. Those eyes, that smile. How had she never noticed those things before? She went straight to the board room, walking in five minutes after the meeting started. A dozen men in high-end suits sat at the conference table, her father, and brothers, Nunzio and Silvestro, among them. Lazaro's eyes followed her as she strode to the head of the table. She cleared her throat, then got straight to business.

"Occhipinti Enterprises is missing out on untapped potential," she began, cueing an aide in the back with a projector. A slide showed an aerial view of the valley, the sprawling Occhipinti vineyards outlined in yellow. A smaller area, nearly adjacent, was shaded red. "It's within our grasp if we dare to take a risk. Today I'm putting things in motion to make it happen."

Two hours later, Chavonne retreated to her office. She closed the door, looking forward to taking a breath after the day's hectic start. On the desk sat a skinny hazelnut mocha, ordered exactly as she had this morning, and piping hot. Next to it was a business card.

DION MAGGIOLI

Executive Officer of Development

Maggioli Garlic Growers

The phone number was circled and there was an arrow pointing to the back of the card. She turned it over and saw a handwritten note.

Here's a replacement for this a.m. Maybe we can enjoy another, together, some time? D.

And then a cell phone number. She eased back in her chair, smiling at the card.

That was a year ago, and they'd shared countless coffees, dinners, and nights since then. He'd taught her about the impact a thriving enterprise could have on a small community like theirs. He always came back to investing in the people who worked for him. Knowing he'd eventually take over the Maggioli garlic empire, he wanted to bring it into the modern age by using AI and automating as much as possible. But his goal was to train the current staff to make and implement those technical improvements. That way no one lost a job, no paycheck went uncollected. The Maggioli employees had been loyal, he reasoned, and he wanted them rewarded for their dedication. He even proposed taking a pay cut to cover the expenses and had been working with Enzo Ferreira to get the board's approval. But Enzo's enthusiasm for the idea had waned, and Dion struggled to gain an ally in his efforts to modernize the family business and make it more profitable for everyone, not just those who shared his last name or sat on the board.

"My grandfather," Dion told her one night while cuddled in bed, "doesn't understand why I offered to cut my pay."

"Neither do I," Chavonne said, nuzzling his chest. "Why should you sacrifice?"

Dion kissed her forehead as he stroked her hair. "Because," he said, "that's what leadership is. Setting an example and showing your staff that you're fully invested in them. Their success is your success, and vice versa. It's good business to repay loyalty with loyalty."

"Loyalty is important in my family," she replied. "We just approach it differently."

Meanwhile, Chavonne tried to convince him that the secrets to success revolved around smashing sales goals and investing in cutting edge equipment. Acquiring as many assets as possible, even if the only benefit of acquisition was keeping said assets unavailable to your competitor. Nunzio and Silvestro had become quite skilled in persuading reluctant investors to "participate," as Lazaro fondly called it, in the success of the Occhipinti wine growing dynasty. A timely visit from her brothers and their associates often resulted in a beneficial transaction to help build the family fortune. She knew how business got done here, but she also knew to keep her hands clean. Lazaro saw to that. After all, she was Daddy's one and only girl. The shining star in his universe. That afforded her luxuries her brothers would never enjoy. And Chavonne was smart enough to look the other way when things didn't concern her or play dumb when necessary. Silicon Valley might be the birthplace of the tech industry. But agriculture built the cradle that nurtured it. And her family, using whatever skills they had available, had earned its place in the hierarchy of the haves. Her father would never allow any family member, most especially his beloved princess, to become one of the have nots.

Chavonne set her journal on the nightstand and took a sip from her wine glass. Then she removed her pink floral silk robe. A long shower, even on a warm summer night like this, would feel good. She pinned up her long brown hair and set the shower heads to pulse.

"Alexa," she instructed, "play Dean Martin."

C'est Magnifique began as Chavonne stepped under the twin streams of water. Old standards always felt right when she was tired. Though holding it together on the outside, she hadn't slept in days. Her neck and back were rigid with tension. She lathered up with a generous dollop of Coco Mademoiselle shower gel, working it over her tanned frame. The jasmine, rose, and patchouli notes scented the steamy air, and she rinsed away the decadent bubbles. Then she directed the jets at her spine and neck, closing her eyes and focusing on Dion's smile as her muscles softened. *Drinking Champagne* began as she shut off the water, refreshed, for now.

"Alexa, skip this song."

Volare cued up and she stepped out of the shower. Her phone beeped as she swaddled herself in an Egyptian cotton towel. She sauntered to her dressing table and checked the screen.

NEED TO MEET. SOON.

Rolling her eyes, she cleared the text. She took another sip of wine, then slipped on a pair of short lavender silk pajamas. Retreating to her bed, she opened her tablet. With a few touches of the screen, she was scrolling through one of her bank accounts. Three deposits in the last two days, right on schedule. Though her family's business kept her comfortable, Chavonne had quietly begun her own enterprise—a property acquisition firm catering to high-end buyers who valued discretion. Silicon Valley was full of them, even here in its south end. And as far as she was concerned, the less the public knew about you, the better.

Her phone beeped again.

DID YOU GET MY LAST TEXT?

She sighed and tapped her reply. CAN'T TALK NOW. TOMORROW AFTERNOON?

She scrolled further down the transactions. It all seemed to be in order. She was setting up a transfer to her savings when the reply came.

1 PM. WINE BAR. SIDEWALK TABLE.

Nope. Too public.

2 PM. WINE BAR. PRIVATE ROOM.

She clicked confirm to send the funds to her savings account.

OK. SEE YOU AT 2.

Instead of a typed reply, she sent back a thumbs-up emoji. Then she returned to her banking and sipped her wine.

Maybe the men in this family will finally learn to take me seriously.

| 7 |

"Mills," Susan whined, "today."

Millie emerged from her lip lock with Pauly, giggling as she pulled away.

"Where you gals going?" Pauly asked, squeezing her rump.

"Exploring," Margaret chimed in. "You boys had your turn. We want to see some sights."

Dom emerged from one of the bedrooms, his salt and pepper hair askew.

"Good morning, sleepyhead," Pauly chided. "What kept you in bed so late?"

Dom shuffled toward the kitchen. "Trying to reach Florence," he replied. "Finally got a reply to my text, but when I asked if I could call, she left me on read."

"Maybe she doesn't feel like talking?" Susan offered.

"Or maybe she can't talk now," Margaret said.

Dom poured a cup of coffee and took a sip. "Maybe," he agreed, "but, it's not like her."

"She's your ex-wife," Margaret reminded. "Totally conceivable that she has other things going on and doesn't have time to talk right now."

"My ex-wife who sent me to find out what happened to her nephew," Dom snapped.

Margaret drew back, "Oh, I didn't mean—"

"I'm sorry," Dom said. "Mags, I shouldn't have come off like that. I apologize."

Margaret waved her hand, "It's okay. I know it's stressful. I shouldn't have come off like that, either. Hopefully, she calls soon."

"I texted her some information we got from the da Conceicaos the other day, but it would be easier to talk it out," Dom said. "Anyway, where are you lovely ladies headed?"

"To learn about the community," Millie said. "There's a museum a few blocks away."

"And shopping," said Margaret.

"Maybe have some wine," added Susan.

Dom and Pauly looked at each other. "Sounds like a good day," Pauly said. He pulled Millie close and kissed her forehead. "You girls be careful."

Millie rolled her eyes, "Why start now?"

"And don't spend all my money," Pauly said, smacking her fanny as she turned, laughing in sync with her sisters as triplets do.

***

They stopped at the plaque outside the museum. "Carnegie Library 1910," Susan read aloud as four elderly men in fedoras passed them on the sidewalk. The last one turned, doffed his hat, and smiled before catching up to the others.

"The steel guy, from New York?" Millie asked, waving to the man.

"Well, he was born in Scotland," Margaret said. "Isn't this town's founder a Scotsman?"

"That's right," Susan said. "The first English-speaking settler."

"But not the *first* settler," Margaret quipped. "That's just an elitist way of saying the first white guy."

"Well, that seems to be the story of our country," Millie said.

The museum was built in the classic revival style, with columns and an ornately carved pediment evoking a Greek temple. Leading up to the double doors was a set of concrete steps, divided by a dark green handrail. Two matching green streetlamps stood at either side.

"Let's see what we can find out," Susan said.

Inside, they were greeted by a white-haired woman wearing a navy sweater and flowy tan trousers. In another time, it would've been easy to picture her as Marlene Dietrich, luxuriating on the deck of a cruise ship and sipping an elderflower martini. "Feel free to look around, and let me know if you have any questions," she invited, waving to the open space of the octagonal rotunda.

The trio browsed various displays, including old photographs of early settlers and artifacts from the region's indigenous people, the Ohlone. Millie stopped at a case of old documents. "Maggioli," she said, "wasn't that the name Dom said Florence gave?"

Margaret walked up, "Yeah, why?"

Millie pointed to a document inside the case. "That name is all over these deeds," she said. "They go way back, some to the 1800s."

"Interesting," Susan noted. "Looks like they own a lot of land here. And there's another familiar name. Da Conceicao. Isn't that the couple the guys visited?"

"Right," Margaret said. "And I see transactions for Ortega, Rosetto, Murphy."

"What's that name?" Susan asked, pointing to a jagged scrawl. "A hundred acres seems like a lot of land, don't you think?"

"Occhi-something," Margaret guessed. "Hard to read."

"Isn't that a wine grower?" Millie asked.

"I think so," Margaret said. "We saw it on the mural when we drove to the house."

"Hey, speaking of wine," Susan said, "you girls ready to get going?"

"It's barely 10:30 in the morning," Millie said.

"Keep your shorts on," Susan laughed. "I was thinking we'd shop first. Then wine."

It was a short walk to the main boulevard, where they entered one of several antique stores that dotted the sidewalk.

"Ooh! Look at these goodies," Margaret trilled as she pawed vintage lingerie. Susan was admiring an old medicine cabinet while Millie examined a pile of books.

"You don't need another negligee," Susan cautioned.

"You don't know that," Margaret laughed, holding up a feather-collared silk robe. "Just because Millie's off the market, and you're determined to live the life of a nun, it doesn't mean I'm not still looking to attract Mr. Right. Or Mr. Right Now."

"In that?" Millie erupted in laughter. "Your old gray caboose ain't where it used t'be."

Margaret cupped her breasts and pushed them upward. "Who said anything about my caboose? No one's gonna be lookin' at that when I've got this on."

"Hey, get a load of this," Susan said, pointing to a large oak barrel standing in the corner. "Occhipinti Vineyards. That's the name on the deeds, right?"

"Established 1913," Millie noted from the stamp on the front of the barrel.

"And this," Margaret pointed to a vintage fruit crate, having torn herself away from the lingerie. "Da Conceicao Growers. The Sweetest Fruits from the Valley of the Heart's Delight."

They moved through the shop, browsing dusty shelves and eyeing old dishes and glassware spilling from time-warped buffets and sideboards in precarious piles. They made their way down the boulevard and popped into a used bookstore. A purring gray and white cat greeted them, wrapping her tail around Susan's leg before jumping up to a shelf in the display window. The store was stacked to the ceiling with shelving units, and each was lined with the spines of books on every subject imaginable. Pungent green carpet spread out in every direction, with little nooks built into the labyrinth of shelving. A soft-shouldered couple, both with long gray hair, conversed at the register, nearly hidden behind a tower of paperbacks.

"Hello," the man said. "First time visiting us?"

Millie nodded, "Yes, this is quite a collection you have here."

"Please feel free to look around and spend as much time as you like," the woman said.

"What do you have on local history?" Susan asked.

"That would be the section behind you," the man said.

Margaret quickly found it and the others followed. The cat laced herself around Susan's leg again as they pored through the shelves.

"You've made a new friend," Millie said.

"That's Lucky," said the man from the counter.

"Well, I can always use a little luck," Susan joked.

"No, I mean her name is Lucky," the man explained. "I think she likes you."

The cat purred as Susan crouched to pat her on the head.

Millie drew her fingers over the books. Garlic Town, read one's spine. It was mostly text, but the middle featured several old photos. "How much is this?"

The man turned the book over. "Eight dollars."

"We'll take it," Millie said. "But I want to look some more."

"Are you interested in the Maggioli family?"

Susan stopped petting the cat and stood up straight. "Why?"

"They're one of the oldest families in town," the man said, walking to the end of the aisle. "If you're interested in local history, you're interested in the Maggiolis. I have a more books about them here."

After browsing the shelves, the girls added three more books to their purchase.

"Here's a punch card," the woman said as she rang up the order on an old register. She held a bright yellow piece of paper, written out by hand. "When you get to ten books, you get fifty percent off the book of your choice. Bring it with you every time you shop."

"Oh, we're just visiting—" Margaret began.

"Thanks," Susan said. "I'm sure we'll be back. Besides, I'll want to see Lucky again."

They waved goodbye and stepped out to the sidewalk.

"Why didn't you want them to know we were visiting?" Margaret asked.

"I'm sure they're nice," Susan said, "but don't you think it's odd that he asked us about the Maggiolis?"

"No," Margaret said. "You were holding a book on garlic. They're garlic growers."

"Right, but when he started talking about local families, he didn't mention any others."

"And that whole display of books about their family, and their family only," Millie pointed out. "Kinda weird, right?"

"Oh," Margaret said, stopping to think it over. "Wait, I still don't get it."

"Like I said, the bookstore owners seem like nice people," Susan said, "but we don't know enough about them. And if a member of the Maggioli family has disappeared, we need to be careful who we talk to. We have no idea who's keeping secrets and who isn't."

Margaret nodded. "Okay, now I get it."

They kept walking, looking in shop windows and admiring the architecture. At the corner was an extravagant building, topped with a majestic clock tower and spire. Red tiles lined the sloping, fairy-tale cottage roof, while the lower levels were made of greystone and white brick. Arched windows stood in rows along the second story. A set of wide steps beckoned visitors, and at the foot stood a bronze statue of the town's founder.

"What's that?" Margaret wondered aloud from their spot across the street.

"That's the old city hall," Susan said. "I saw a picture of it when we were in the museum earlier. Now it's a restaurant."

They continued up the block, greeted by delicious aromas from several eateries. "You gals getting hungry?" Millie asked.

"Sure," Susan said. "How about this café?"

They looked inside to see tables packed with people.

Susan frowned. "Okay, maybe not."

"Oh, here we go," Margaret announced, pointing to a round sign protruding from a building further up the street.

Wine Bar.

"Perfect," Susan said. "Just what we need."

As they walked through the tiny courtyard terrace, Millie noticed the four elderly gentlemen in fedoras sitting at one of the stone tables, a glass of wine in front of each of them.

"Didn't we see those guys earli—"

But before she could finish, Margaret pulled her inside. It was dimly lit for this sunny afternoon. A white-aproned waiter approached from behind the long, gleaming bar.

"Good afternoon, ladies," he said with a dimpled smile. "I'm Jeremy. Will you be joining us for lunch, or just a glass of wine today?"

"Lunch, please," Susan said. "A table for three."

"Of course, right this way," he said, ushering them down a narrow hallway, lined with framed wine labels and a collection of black and white photos featuring the area's vineyards.

"Can we sit in here?" Millie asked as she passed a room off the hallway. A young, sharply dressed woman with highlighted brown hair looked up from a small table along the far wall. She was seated across from a man whose back was to the doorway. The woman glared.

"Oh, I'm afraid that's a private room," Jeremy said, pulling the door closed and continuing down the hallway. "But how's this?"

He gestured to a tall table with three stools. Susan frowned.

"Do you have anything a little closer to the ground? It's a little tricky to hoist our keisters up on these barstools at our age. Gravity isn't exactly our friend."

"Oh, of course," Jeremy said. "Would you be more comfortable here?" He showed them to a wide black leather booth lined with dark cherry wood, then distributed menus.

"Perfect," the trio said in unison as they took their seats.

"What do you recommend?" Susan asked.

"Well, for lunch, we have several wood-fired pizza options and a selection of salads. All from fresh, local ingredients, of course. And to drink, I can recommend anything based on your preferences, but," he looked toward the hallway, "I highly suggest you try the Occhipinti Vineyards Petit Syrah if you like a nice red. And if you prefer a white, I'd steer you toward the Occhipinti Vineyards Pinot Grigio."

"Jeremy, is that the only wine you carry, Occhipinti Vineyards?" Millie asked.

"Oh, no," he said with a nervous laugh, "it's just, *in my opinion,* the best choice. In fact, I can set you up with a little tasting if you like. But we do have many other wines to choose from."

"All right," Susan said. "How about three glasses of the Petit Syrah to get us started?"

"Excellent choice," he said.

"And then we'll do a tasting of—what do you think, girls? Let's say four?"

Margaret and Millie nodded in agreement.

"Very well," Jeremy said. When he left, Millie craned her neck toward the terrace.

"What?" Margaret asked.

"I *know* those are the guys we saw outside the museum," Millie said.

"So? They probably walked over here like we did," Susan said from behind her menu. "Cripes, how does anyone charge $24 for a pizza? And 'New York style?' My ass. I bet it's like a communion wafer with cheap sausage. Can't even fold it."

"Prosciutto and goat cheese tells me everything I need to know," Margaret quipped as she scanned the listings. "Fig spread? Who puts that on a pizza? With a balsamic glaze?"

"Our homemade vinaigrette features the finest garlic from Maggioli Garlic Growers," Susan quoted. "I get the feeling it would be considered a sin to use anything else in this town. The Maggiolis and the Occhipintis seem to have quite an influence."

"Do you think they're following us?" Millie asked.

"You're being paranoid," Margaret said. "They were here before us, remember? If anything, we're following them."

"Maybe we should sit outside," Millie persisted.

Susan closed her menu. "Really, Mills?" She narrowed her eyes and peered out the front window. "You know, that one guy is kinda cute."

Margaret whipped her head around, "Which one? The one in the hat?"

"They're all wearing hats," Susan said. "The one with the blue shirt, on the left."

"It's eighty degrees. Why are they all wearing long sleeves?" Margaret wondered.

"Because some gentlemen still understand how to dress," Millie said.

"Now that you mention it, I do like the look of the one in the grey fedora," Margaret said.

As Jeremy returned with their wine, Millie said, "I'm sorry. Can we sit outside?"

He frowned as Susan cut in, "And we'll have one pizza margherita, one watermelon and arugula salad, and one—"

"Prosciutto and goat cheese pizza," Margaret said as they stood to gather their things.

Millie snickered and shot Susan a glance.

Jeremy nodded. "Of course, ladies. I'll have it all sent out there so you can enjoy your meal and wine tasting *al fresco.*"

As they walked down the hallway, raised voices came from inside the private room. "If I want something done, I have to do it myself," they heard the woman say as another waiter hurried to pull the door closed. "Wouldn't be the first time."

The triplets sat at a table across from the men in fedoras. Jeremy served their wine and went back inside. The man in the blue shirt tipped his hat to Millie. She waved, turning her hand to show her wedding ring. When she nodded toward Susan, the man offered Susan a smile.

"Good afternoon, ladies," he said, raising his wine glass.

"Good afternoon," they replied in unison.

"Lovely weather," said the one in the grey fedora, turning to look at them.

"Yes, it certainly is," Margaret said.

"Are you triplets?" a third man at the table asked.

"We are," they said, again in unison. This caused all seven of them to chuckle.

"I'm Ottavio Tremolada," said the one in the grey fedora. "They call me Eight Ball."

"Bartolomeo Zanetti," said the man with his back to the wall, raising his hand.

"Eufrasio Volpe," said the third man as he doffed his hat. Millie recognized him as the man she'd waved to at the museum.

"And I am Fortunato Giardi," said the one in blue, focused on Susan. He was tall and wide in all the right places, filling out his shirt like a high school quarterback. He had dusky skin, a full head of white hair, and a gleaming Pepsodent smile. "But my friends call me Lucky."

She blushed. "Well, that's odd. You're the second Lucky I've met today."

Never mind that the first one was a cat.

"If that's the case, *cara mia*, it must be your Lucky Day," he said, his cobalt eyes—deep as the Mediterranean—twinkling.

They all broke out laughing again as their food arrived. Susan, always the level-headed one—after all, she was born three minutes before Margaret and eight before Millie—had now transformed into a cloying schoolgirl. Millie leaned over and gently patted Susan's lap.

"Get it together," she whispered through a plastered-on smile.

"I can't help it," Susan said as she brought her wine glass to her lips. "He's such a silver fox. And those eyes. They're the duck's nuts."

Lucky raised his glass to Susan, who reciprocated.

"Yeah, well, those nuts aren't what we're here for," Millie said.

"Speak for yourself, sister," Susan quipped.

Margaret dabbed her lips with a napkin. "So, are you fellas regulars here?"

Eight Ball shrugged. "Yes," he said, "but we could say that about a lot of places."

"And there's nothin' regular about Eight Ball," Lucky said with a deep laugh. Eufrasio and Bartolomeo chuckled in their softer tones.

"What's your interest in the Maggiolis?" Lucky asked.

"What?" Susan froze, holding a forkful of watermelon. "Why do you ask?"

"That book," Lucky said, motioning to the bag from the bookstore on the fourth chair. "That's what it's about, the Maggioli family."

"Oh," she said, flustered. "We just wanted to learn about the local history."

"Not from here, are you?" Eight Ball asked.

"We're visiting a friend," Margaret lied.

"Anyone we know?" Eight Ball tried.

Margaret shifted, "Oh, I don't know if we should say."

"Ottavio," Eufrasio said, "don't be a creep. Respect the ladies' privacy, huh?" Then he turned to the triplets. *"Vi chiedo scusa, signore*—I beg your pardon, ladies—sometimes these guys forget their manners."

There was an awkward silence, and finally Lucky said, "But if you really want to know about the Maggiolis, you won't learn the real story in that book. That family has a lot of secrets. And they're not the only family in this town with something to hide."

* * *

"Ostriches?" Dom asked, jotting down the information on a notepad. "You sure?"

"Yeah," Pauly said, eyes glued to his phone. "It says ostriches and farm animals."

Dom smoothed his tropical-patterned shirt and patted his pockets a second time before finally locating the keys to the rental car. "And why are we going out there again?"

"To be one with nature," Pauly said. "Why sit here and let the girls have all the fun?"

"Ugh, nature is hot and makes me sweat," Dom said.

Pauly handed him a straw trilby, the same hat all the elders in the old neighborhood wore to outdoor functions. The symbol that marked entry into the senior generation. "Put this on," he said, pulling on one of his own. "You look sharp."

"Sharp like a bowlin' ball," Dom quipped.

"Shuddup," Pauly said, smacking his arm. "You got the directions?"

"Yeah, just outside town, past the fruit stands."

As they eased up the winding hillsides, they passed several produce markets, each with weathered wooden shacks and spray-painted signs advertising their wares.

"Bada-Bing Cherries," Dom chuckled as they drove past a stand. "Get it? Bing cherries? Bada-*Bing*? That's perfect for a coupla fellas like us, huh? We gotta stop there on the way back."

Minutes later, Pauly pulled into the ostrich farm's dusty lot, parking by a large barn.

"Madonn', they really got ostriches," Dom observed, pointing to several pens situated in the back, where the flat land eased into craggy foothills. "Out here in the middle of nowhere."

"Told you."

They walked into the converted barn, which housed a gift shop plus several exotic reptiles and other small animals. After paying for two tickets, they were given cups of feed for the animals.

"Just watch yourself," the skinny teenager slouched over the cash register told them as he slipped his earbuds back in. "They run really fast and can get aggressive."

"I ain't afraid of no giant birds," Dom scoffed as they stepped into the sunshine.

"Got the place to ourselves," Pauly noted, looking around the otherwise people-free farm.

They passed enclosures of rabbits, miniature horses, chickens, pot-bellied pigs, goats, and sheep as they crossed the dirt to the ostrich pens. Several black and white birds—males, according to the kid in the barn—were crowded against the railing of their pens, bobbing their long necks and bristling against each other.

"Guess they smell the food," Pauly said, shaking one of his cups. Nearby, a group of smaller, pale brown ostriches were clustered in another pen. "Those must be the females."

Dom watched the males jostle for position. "I'd get irritated to be kept away from the ladies, too. Look at all that tail," he joked, noting their plumage.

"And yet so close," Pauly said. "Look at what you can't have, right in front of you."

"The blue ball effect," Dom chuckled as he held out a cup. The birds swarmed and darted, pecking their beaks inside and spilling pellets on the ground. Their long lashes fluttered over glassy, orb-like eyes. Some hissed.

"Whoa," Pauly said stepping back. "Calm down, ladies. There's enough for everyone."

Dom ambled to the other pen. Four of the males immediately breezed up to him, sticking their necks over the bars. "I got you, fellas," he said as the three others clustered around. He held the cups out at arm's length, and like the females, they dove toward the cups. "Easy now, easy."

The two largest ostriches stood side by side, fanning out their black and white feathers and then dropping their heads to puff out their necks. A few warbly tones followed, and then they traded throaty booms, as if competing.

"What in the honking bassoon fuck," Dom wondered aloud, suddenly feeling threatened.

Pauly laughed as the ostriches postured and lowered their necks to make the bass sounds.

"It ain't funny, Pauly," Dom said, afraid to move. "I think they wanna hurt me."

"You know how dumb that looks?" Pauly said between chuckles.

The breeze kicked up suddenly, blowing Dom's trilby off his head. He watched with horror as it sailed into the pen. Then he squatted to see if he could reach it through the fence, but it was too far away. The ostriches swarmed and began pecking at it. Instinctively, Dom stepped onto the bottom rung of the fence, hoping for a better look. Then he climbed the second and third rung. He was as tall as the ostriches now, knees even with the top of the fence.

"Dom, what are you—" Pauly began as Dom slipped and fell over the top, his face and chest skidding into the dirt. The ostriches' long, muscular legs surrounded him, as if he'd landed in an abandoned fairy-tale forest. Unbothered, they continued to peck at his trilby, sending bits of straw into the air. Meanwhile, the female ostriches bobbed, hissing as Pauly ran to the pen.

Dom was stuck in soft, sand-like dirt that offered no leverage. But as Pauly climbed the fence, the largest male lunged at him. Trying to avoid the bird, he lost his balance and crashed into the dirt.

"Oh shit," Dom said, scrambling on hands and knees like a bear as a large male nipped his buttocks. He raced to the fence and tried to squeeze through but didn't fit. With half his gut draped over the bottom rung, he flailed and kicked as the ostrich continued to peck at his behind. His shirt pushed up past his belly, searing his skin on the hot metal. "Get it offa me!"

Pauly waved maniacally to distract the bird. As Dom gasped for breath, Pauly ran the other way, hoping the bird would follow. That seemed like a good plan, until it worked.

Because once it went after Pauly, so did the others. Wedged between the rungs, Dom squealed and cursed. Pauly heard the footfalls of seven ostriches close in. He raced across the pen, hoping to reach the far end before the ostriches could catch up to him. A few steps from the fence, he rolled his ankle and slid awkwardly. The males were making the low, throaty sounds now. Honking and bobbing their necks as they sprinted after him. In a desperate lunge, Pauly reached the fence and hopped onto the second rung. As he flung himself over the top, the ostriches jammed together at the fence, their long necks swooping toward him.

"Help!" Dom squealed like a little girl. "My stomach is burning!"

Pauly dropped to his knees and reached for Dom's arms. Grasping him just below the armpits, he yanked, but Dom wouldn't budge.

"OOF!" Dom yelled as Pauly tried again, this time from a squat. "My guts!"

The ostriches' honking grew louder as they approached.

"Come on, Dom," Pauly said, giving a mighty tug. The hot metal had reddened the skin on Dom's belly as he tried to wriggle free. "Work with me, huh?"

"I'm tryin'," Dom said, "Madonn', you don't think I'm tryin'?"

With a Herculean pull, Pauly finally dislodged Dom from the fence, just as the ostriches began to plunge their necks into Dom's ample backside. Tangled together, the men tumbled down the hill. At last, they came to rest against the gate to the goat pen. Sitting up and taking inventory, Dom ran a thick hand over his burnt, chafed stomach. "Thought I was a goner," he gasped. "Thank you, my friend."

Pauly gathered himself, leaning on the gate as he exhaled. "You mean to tell me, we survived all those years in the, uh, *lifestyle*, lammed off all dem johns, dodged I dunno how many bullets, and it was about to be Death by Ostrich? That's how two goombahs go out?"

Dom managed a weak chuckle before grabbing his side. "Not the way I thought I'd go."

"It never is," Pauly said, erupting into a hearty laugh. But as he did, the gate gave way and the pair fell onto their backs. Almost immediately, a passel of rambunctious goats bounced out of the pen. With hearty bleats, they trounced in every direction, climbing on various large rocks and leaping off to form a stampede.

"Oh my God," Dom said, crossing himself, "what have we done?"

Pauly put his hands atop his head, confounded to silence.

"Hey!" called a voice from the barn. The kid with the earbuds ran after the goats and, miraculously, rounded them up. "Get in there!" He held the gate open as they filed in. Then he slammed it shut. "You all right?"

"Yeah," Pauly said, "fine. Thanks. I guess I slipped and fell against the gate. Sorry."

"Eh, don't worry about it," the kid said, testing the gate to be sure it was closed. "I keep telling the owner they need to repair these gates. Why don't you guys come in and get something to drink? It's hot out here."

They walked back to the barn in silence, reliving their little adventure in their heads, as the ostriches pecked apart the remnants of Dom's trilby.

"Here," the kid said, reaching into the cooler to pull out three bottles of water.

Dom, sweaty and sticky, chugged the icy water and let it cool his parched throat. The sun had beat down on his now hatless head and he felt like he might overheat.

"So, are you guys visiting?" the kid asked.

"Yeah," Pauly said.

"From where?"

With ease, Pauly slipped back into wise guy mode. "Out of town," he said succinctly.

The kid sipped his water. "I see."

"Hey," Dom said, hoping to change the subject, "how did this place get here? I mean, who puts ostriches out in the middle of nowhere?"

The kid laughed. "Weird, I know. The Occhipintis own this land."

Dom's brow lifted. "The wine growers?"

"Yeah, but obviously, you can't grow grapes out here. Or anything, really."

"Not even garlic?" Pauly asked.

The kid took another swig of his water and laughed. "Nah, man. That's what people think. But my mom works in the city clerk's office. And," he looked over his shoulder, "the Maggiolis don't own much land."

"How do you run a garlic empire without owning the land?" Dom wondered.

Leaning over the counter, the kid said, "They rent most of it. The Occhipintis practically own this whole town."

| 8 |

"Italy?" Kate Kendall asked. "How can that be?"

"The trip was scheduled in March," said the voice on the line, "and he can't be reached."

An abrupt click ended the conversation.

"Why would Carlo Maggioli leave the country so soon after his son's death?" she mused to Peaches, curled up to snooze in the bay window. Kate opened a document on her laptop and started flipping the pages of her notebook. "Let's see if we can connect some dots."

Highlighter in hand, she went through her notes, marking anything to do with Carlo. For years, it remained a mystery as to what transgression had been so serious to remove him from the family business. It takes hardy stock to survive in agriculture, and the Maggiolis were a tough bunch. But publicly, they did and said the right things. Ignazio, the patriarch, seemed shrewd yet kindly. Dion, on the few occasions she'd met him, was compassionate and exuberant. But Carlo was forever brooding, as if burdened with some unforgivable sin.

There was a notable aloofness to him, more than a proverbial chip on his shoulder. It was nearly a defiant embrace of his role as the family outcast. Even his long, rock star hair said "anti-establishment." And yet it was painfully obvious that all he sought in life was his father's approval and acceptance. Though he appeared with his family at public events, he was rarely mentioned. His name vanished from the company org chart. Quietly removed from the board more than twenty years ago, not long after Dion was born. No explanation was given. Many assumed he and Ignazio had a falling out, but even so, that seemed a severe punishment.

Shortly afterward, Gloria Maggioli was thrown from her horse while out for a morning ride along the foothill ridge bordering their property. She tumbled dozens of feet and landed violently in a ravine. When she hadn't returned in time to nurse Dion, Carlo mounted his own horse and went looking for her. Those were the days before cell phones. He was horrified when he found her, bleeding and barely conscious, her pelvis smashed. He raced back to their estate to call for help. An ambulance arrived within minutes, but the sprawling property's craggy terrain made it impossible to reach her. A helicopter was then dispatched and, in shock and losing blood at a rapid rate, she was eventually air lifted to the hospital.

They tried to keep that quiet, too, Kate had learned through research, but couldn't. Gloria Maggioli was in the hospital for more than a month. She'd suffered multiple fractures and needed four operations before she could learn to walk again. Carlo retreated even further into seclusion. Obsessed with keeping his family safe, nearly to the point of paranoia. Work trucks were seen at the family estate at all hours. As technology evolved, so did their security systems. Carlo installed cameras, fencing, and motion-sensing lights. Additional structures were built, rumored to house full-time caregivers, tutors, domestic servants, and anyone else who worked on the property. Their mansion and gardens, set high on a hill overlooking South County's fertile acreage, became a compound.

In restaurants, he'd sit by himself, and request that no one be seated near him. Easier to insulate himself from the whispered conversations that took place among the business crowd. He dabbled in philanthropy, making donations to various charities benefitting local children. But he rarely appeared at events, instead sending funds electronically and a form letter. Even his foundation seemed to be nothing more than a ghost company. A post office box and out of service phone number were the only contacts. At night, he was occasionally spotted at a seedy sports bar, holed up in his own booth and downing Manhattans until either his credit card or his cognition gave out.

Meanwhile, Carlo didn't seem to have a job. Although he'd been ousted from the family business, he hadn't been cut off financially. How else would he be able to pay for Gloria's medical bills, not to mention all the improvements to the property? Surely, Ignazio hadn't shunned him completely. Blood still counted for something among the Maggioli family. But the mystery of his departure from the garlic growing empire, and the source of his income, persisted. She'd heard rumors that he was loansharking some of the smaller businesses in town but couldn't confirm anything. Besides, every business was a smaller business compared to Maggioli Garlic Growers. Except, of course, Occhipinti Vineyards. And there seemed to be a code of silence when it came to discussing questionable finances.

Peaches uncurled her tail and began to knead the cushion on the window seat. Kate opened her browser and pulled up the newspaper's archives.

MAGGIOLI, she typed into the search bar, CARLO.

Hundreds of hits unfurled on her screen. In the search bar, she typed BUSINESS HOLDINGS. The results narrowed to about sixty. She looked out the window, catching a glimpse of the clock tower atop Old City Hall. Then she typed PUBLIC NOTICES 1990-2000. When the results appeared, she scanned the list, then leaned forward, squinting in disbelief.

"Well, well," she said, clicking on a link near the bottom, "I wasn't expecting this."

* * *

Rialta Occhipinti used her delicate fingertips to pat a high-end European moisturizer into her skin. She took a long look in the mirror. A few crow's feet and fine lines, she observed, but not bad. Now in her early fifties, she still had the glowing complexion of a woman half her age. With a silver-handled boar bristle brush, she smoothed her waist-length black hair. One hundred strokes each morning, that was one of her secrets. With high cheekbones, deep green eyes, and impossibly white teeth, she didn't need much in the way of makeup. In fact, when she met Lazaro on the beach in Positano, he remarked that no cosmetic could improve on her perfect features. That was thirty years ago, and he sealed the deal by taking her to La Sponda that evening. He'd reserved the entire restaurant, lit only by hundreds of candles, for an intimate dinner in the heart of the Italian riviera. Smitten immediately, she never left his side.

Her family had made their money in banking; some whispered that heads conveniently turned the other way when Mussolini came into power and fascists manipulated both prices and wages. But that was her parents' generational shame, not her concern. Rialta was fascinated by horticulture. She liked the idea of tending the earth to provide for mankind. Her parents indulged her interest and sent her to school in Florence, poorly disguising their hopes that she'd find a husband more than earn a degree. What could become of a woman with a love for plants? A studious Italian businessman with Gucci loafers and a sensible retirement plan would suit them nicely. But she'd come to enjoy the freedom of living away from her parents' expectations.

Athletic and statuesque, she'd studied ballet and earned praise on the volleyball court as a schoolgirl, with no intention of pursuing either activity beyond college. She took modeling jobs between classes and received plenty of attention from her fellow undergrads. But none were dynamic enough to capture her interest. After graduation, she ventured to Positano. Something about the turquoise waters and salty air refreshed her unencumbered spirit.

And there was Lazaro, barrel-chested and luxuriously tan, soaking up the Mediterranean sun with all the confidence of Cary Grant. *Mia Sofia,* he called her—noting her resemblance to a young Sophia Loren. Both intrigued and somewhat repelled by his American swagger, she perked up when he said his Californian family was in the agricultural business. The fact that he spoke nearly fluent Italian only enhanced his irrepressible charm.

Three decades on, she found herself competing for his attention. It wasn't that the fire had gone out; they still enjoyed intimacy and gestures of courtship. But life in viticulture could be all consuming. He traveled frequently, inspected grapes from the family's vineyards, met with representatives of retailers and restaurants, and monitored the company's finances. As the head of such a prestigious industry, he was also expected to contribute to the community. Corporate gifts and donations improved the Occhipinti image, one he'd cultivated as meticulously as the *Carignano* grapes his family's vineyards had become known for. Said to be brought over from Sardinia, Rialta—like all the Occhipintis—knew it was in fact the Carignane grape, a native California varietal, that had flourished in this terroir and given their wine its distinct flavor. But, as the Occhipintis liked to say, why let a little thing like the truth ruin a good story?

"Wine is not just a libation," Lazaro professed one evening while courting her. He'd flown her to the family vineyard in this golden-hued valley, and her eyes widened as they passed symmetrical rows dappled by the evening light. "Wine is an experience, an immeasurable blessing, and the blood of life itself. The grapes we grow serve more than ourselves. They become part of a family's history, poured at joyous events, raised in honor of those lost, providing solace in times of reflection, for generations. It is our duty to make them worthy."

Rialta set her brush down and checked the slim diamond-bordered face of her Jaeger-LeCoultre watch. Nearly half past seven. She'd need to hurry to make the chamber breakfast. With the harvest gala coming up, it was necessary to attend community events and promote the family business. A forest green suit, the jacket nipped at the waist and the skirt skimming her knees, accentuated her frame. She pinned on a sparkling gold and diamond brooch shaped like a cluster of grapes, found a pair of matching pumps, and glided down the wrought iron staircase.

"Good morning," greeted Hesperia, the Occhipintis' housekeeper, lifting a breakfast tray.

"Good morning," Rialta said, pulling her keys from her clutch purse. "I'm having breakfast at the chamber. Has anyone picked up my dry cleaning?"

Hesperia's face sagged as she lowered the tray. "No ma'am, but it's on my list today."

"Good," Rialta said, pushing her hair back before pulling on a chic pair of tortoiseshell cat-eye sunglasses. "I'll be back in about two hours. Then I need to meet with Mr. Occhipinti to go over details for the harvest gala."

"He's already left for the office, Mrs. O—"

"Yes, Hesperia, I'm aware," Rialta said as she checked her lipstick in the mirror. "We'll both be here for lunch. And please, not another cobb salad. Ugh, I'm late."

With that, she whisked out the door and into her silver Jaguar roadster. Fifteen minutes later, she was taking her seat at the head table, thinking about what she'd say in her presentation. It seemed she'd been doing these tedious events for decades and could rattle off the virtues of Occhipinti Vineyards in her sleep. After a dreadful cup of coffee, a stale croissant, and damp scrambled eggs, she stepped to the podium.

"Good morning," she said, her forged, gleaming smile in place. Though she'd been an American citizen for a quarter of a century, she found it helpful to let her native accent slip back into her speech for events such as this. "It's my pleasure to be with you today. At Occ-h-i-pin-ti (she drew it out to punctuate each syllable) Vineyards, we have been working hard to bring you a boun-ti-ful har-vest. And we hope you'll join us in celebration next month at our annual ga-la…"

An hour and twenty minutes later, she was back in her Jag. She pulled an Hermès scarf from the glove compartment, fastened it around her hair, then dropped the top. After giving a courtesy wave to the cluster of sensible-shoed ladies in summery frocks gathered at the curb to wrap up stray chamber business—a precursor to small town gossip—Rialta shot into traffic.

Pulling into the driveway of the estate, she spied Lazaro on the phone. She inched the Jag into its garage space and tucked her scarf into the glove box.

"See that it gets done, Silvestro," Lazaro snapped as he hung up and opened her door.

"Buongiorno, mia Sofia," he said, offering his hand, which she accepted. Then he kissed her angular cheek. "You look beautiful today. How was the rotary meeting?"

"Chamber breakfast," she purred, offering him the other cheek, "and it was ghastly, as always. What's going on with Silvestro?"

He held the door to the house open for her. "I need him to close a real estate deal."

"I thought that was Chavonne's project," Rialta said. "Why do you take it out of her hands? She's more than capable."

He sighed, *"Cara,* you two sound like a broken record. I asked Silvestro to handle this transaction, and I want him to follow through."

"But Chavonne knows more about real estate," Rialta countered, retrieving a bottle of Pellegrino from the stainless refrigerator. She handed it to him and then pulled out one for herself. "She should handle it."

Lazaro uncapped the bottles and poured each one into a tall crystal glass before they moved to his office. "Silvestro and Nunzio have been working on it for a while," he explained. "It's only fair that they finish it."

She stretched her long legs onto the leather couch across from his desk and twirled her hair in her fingers. "You should have given it to Chavonne in the first place," she said, "but, you'll know better next time."

"She was busy," Lazaro said. "Always off with her boyfriend."

The mood soured and Rialta ran her finger over the rim of her glass. "Fiancé," she corrected. "Dion was her *fiancé.*"

"I never saw a ring," Lazaro countered.

"He wanted her to pick it out," Rialta said, smoothing her hair. "For all intents and purposes, they were engaged. And we could've announced it at the harvest gala if he hadn't …"

Lazaro frowned. "I know," he said. "I'll be honest, Dion Maggioli is not the man I would've chosen for Chavonne. But he made her happy."

Rialta set her glass down and put her head in her hands. "It's all so sad," she said. "And crazy. He was so young and vibrant. I can't believe he's dead."

Lazaro shook his head and shrugged. "I know. And I have a bad feeling about this."

"Why do you say that?" Rialta asked, raising her head.

"I know the Maggiolis have kept things quiet, but from what I'm hearing, I don't think his death was an accident," he said, lowering his voice. "You know I don't trust Carlo."

"You don't think that he … *His own son?*"

"I won't rule it out," Lazaro said. "His past is shady, and we know how to handle undesirable elements. He's always resented us for donating land for the community college, putting our name on something to serve future generations. But more than that, he got sauced on a cocktail of misplaced confidence and unchecked ambition. Too proud to acknowledge his mistake."

"Mistake?" Rialta questioned, taken aback by her husband's brusque insensitivity.

"You can call it something else if you want. But that cockiness led him to make some *ill-informed decisions* when he was on the board at Maggioli Garlic Growers, let's say."

Rialta twirled her hair again. "You mean selling those deeds to your family? Forcing his family to rent back their own land?"

Lazaro sipped his water, seeming to relish the thought. "I'm not saying it didn't benefit us. And not selling. *Loaning.* That was the arrangement. And that loan is coming due soon."

Rialta sat back on the couch, her emerald eyes flitting to the collection of Renaissance art behind her husband's desk. Prominently displayed was a reproduction of Filippino Lippi's *Madonna with Child and Saints*. Its bold blues and reds nearly overshadowed the image of the sleeping infant on his mother's lap. "You and Carlo were friendly at one time," she said.

"Yes, but loyalty comes at a price." He opened a drawer and pulled out a slim revolver.

"Lazaro—"

He held up his hand, silencing her. "Questionable behavior," he said, checking the chamber, "has a way of coming back to haunt you. And you must choose carefully who you trust with your secrets. I don't know anything solid, but I think we should prepare."

"Prepare? For what?"

His eyes flashed. "War."

| 9 |

Ignazio Maggioli tapped his fingers on the desk. He was not a man accustomed to waiting. The bank officer returned, an apologetic smile on her face as she closed the door.

"I'm sorry to keep you waiting," she said, sitting in her chair. "I had to verify some information and … there's an obstacle."

Ignazio leaned forward, his silvered brow aloft. *"Obstacle?"*

A nervous laugh escaped as she blanched. "Yes, well, Mr. Maggioli, I'm not sure how it happened, but it looks like there are insufficient funds in the account."

"You're telling me that account has a negative balance?"

Another nervous laugh, as if she couldn't help it. "As I said, I'm not sure how—"

"Let me speak to your superior," Ignazio said, filmy eyes fixed on her until she squirmed.

"That's just it, Mr. Maggioli," she explained, "I'm the superior officer at this branch."

His eyes narrowed. Irritated, he spoke in low, measured tones. "My grandson was the account holder. As you are aware since I provided a death certificate, he is now deceased. I urge you to keep that information confidential as the Maggioli family does not wish to publicize his death. But we do need to regain control of that account and find out where that money went. So please tell me how you can resolve that for me today."

"I'm afraid that would be a breach of protocol, Mr. Maggioli," she said. "You see, you're not listed as an account holder on that account."

"It belongs to a Maggioli Garlic Growers corporate official," he cut in.

"Yes, technically, that's correct," she said, swallowing hard. "But that doesn't matter if you're not listed on the account."

"So, no one else can access it?"

"Only the co-account holder," she said, shrinking in her chair.

"Co-account holder? Who would that be?"

"I'm not at liberty to share that information," she said.

He sat back, sizing her up. She laid one hand over the other to disguise a tremble. "You make good money here, Miss ..." his eyes turned to the nameplate on her desk, "Garcia?"

She shook her head slowly, "I'm ... I'm not sure why you'd ask that. I—"

"Branch management should pay well. Are you comfortable?"

An awkward silence followed. "I don't see what that has to do with this, Mr. Maggioli."

"This bank has been around for quite a while," he mused. "I remember when it first opened. One of the first businesses in what we now call the downtown corridor. This bank's founder, Neville Shaw—God rest his soul—approached me personally. We'd been using a larger bank but wanted to keep our money local and invest in the community. By doing so, we encouraged other agricultural families to use this bank. Sort of how one hand washes the other, you know? Our success is your success and vice versa." He leaned over again and patted his hand against her desk to emphasize the following words, "It would be a shame if Maggioli Garlic Growers were to pull *every goddamn cent we have* out of your institution, Miss Garcia."

Her cheek twitched as he waited for her to speak.

"Mr. Maggioli," she finally said, "it is against our policy to reveal the identity of account holders to anyone who is not listed on the account. I'm sure you can appreciate the concern over privacy, and I'd like to remind you that our privacy policy protects you as well."

He stared but could see his efforts to intimidate her weren't working. Seamlessly shifting gears, he picked up the framed photo on the corner of her desk. Inside was an image of the bank supervisor and a young girl.

"Miss Garcia," he said, running his fingers over the frame. "I hope you will reconsider. I would hate to see something happen to you. Looks like you're a good mother. And your bank needs my company's business."

Again, her cheek twitched as her eyes darted to the photo.

There it was.

Gingerly, as if handling a baby bird, he set the frame back on her desk.

"I will see what I can do," she said, her voice quivering.

He waved his hand and nodded. "It would be much appreciated, Miss Garcia."

She tapped at her keyboard, glancing to the window that looked out to the branch's lobby and then back to her computer screen. Ignazio kept his eyes directly on her, never releasing his gaze. Finally, she picked up a pen and a piece of paper, then set it down. Nervously, her eyes darted to the window again. Then she reached into her purse for her cell phone and began typing in her note app. When she was done, she turned the screen toward Ignazio.

C. OCCHIPINTI

He read it multiple times to be sure but remained expressionless. She raised her brows and nodded slowly. When he nodded in return, she erased the screen.

"Miss Garcia," he said as they both stood up, "I appreciate your time today." He checked his watch and continued, "Please give my best to Emiliana. She should be getting out of class at Sainte Cecelia's right about now, walking home down Myrtle Avenue. And of course, I wish to extend my gratitude for keeping this matter between us. You've been most helpful."

Knees wobbling, she clutched the edge of her desk, stuffing her breath until he left.

He crossed the parking lot and entered the back of a black sedan. "Sergio," he said, "take me to my office." From behind a tinted window, he scowled as they passed the wine bar.

They're going to regret this.

* * *

Nunzio Occhipinti looked up from his cell phone. "Silvestro," he called to his brother across the gym, "Pops wants us to get ready."

Silvestro finished his biceps curls and admired himself in the mirror. "For what?"

Nunzio walked up and whispered, "To send a message."

Silvestro pushed his backwards black ballcap away from his forehead and chugged a protein shake. "What kinda message?"

Nunzio looked around. The gym was nearly empty, but he wanted to be sure. "The kind someone doesn't forget. Come on. We can take my truck."

* * *

GARLIC BRAIDS
GARLIC ICE CREAM
FRESH PRODUCE
HOMEMADE PIES
GIFTS

Pauly and Millie navigated the hand-painted signs lining the dirt lot and pulled up to the large farm stand bordering Bel Monte Boulevard, a few blocks from Occhipinti Community College.

"Garlic ice cream?" Millie sniffed. "Sounds disgusting."

"People will eat anything if they think it's fancy," he said, lacing his fingers inside hers. A large black 4x4 truck barreled through the lot, narrowly missing them. Pauly instinctively directed Millie out of its path.

"Guess those two were in a hurry," she said.

"Maybe they didn't want their garlic ice cream to melt," Pauly joked. "You all right?"

"Fine," she said. "So brave of you to protect me."

"Can't let anything happen to you, baby," he said.

The truck merged onto the road, toward the setting sun. Inside the stand, ripe tomatoes were artfully arranged in a crimson pyramid. Mounds of apricots the color of summer sunsets sweetly scented the air. In the center of the stand was a huge display of garlic. Papery-sheathed cloves spilled from bushel baskets onto a countertop. Jars of pickled, chopped, and minced garlic lined either side. Braided bulbs hung from the display's frame. All bearing the name Maggioli.

"Can I help you?" asked a young woman piling lemons into a bin.

"Oh, we're just looking," Millie said.

"How is this Maggioli garlic?" Pauly wanted to know. "What's so special about it?"

She shrugged. "It's the only garlic we sell, grown right here in this valley. Family's been growing it forever."

"Nice family?" Pauly pressed.

"The Maggiolis?" She let out a slight chuckle. "We don't really travel in the same circles, but they do a lot for the community."

Pauly got the feeling she was reading a script.

"In fact," she continued, "one of them usually comes by around this time to stock the cooler in the back. Used to be the grandson, but I haven't seen him for weeks."

"The cooler?" Millie asked.

"The grandson?" Pauly wondered aloud.

"For garlic?" they said together.

"For the ice cream," the clerk said. "And pies."

"Garlic … *pies?*" Pauly asked, contorting his face.

"Fruit pies, from another farm," the young woman explained, "but I think they're all related. Cousins maybe? I don't know. But they're made with fruit from local orchards."

"Not garlic," Pauly reassured himself.

A woman, the only other customer, approached the counter with two baskets of cherries. "Look around and let me know if you have any questions. But we're closing in a few minutes."

Pauly and Millie strolled the aisles, holding hands and looking at the array of produce.

"You know," she said, rubbing his arm, "we haven't had much alone time since we got here. I'm glad we had the chance to escape for a bit."

Pauly squeezed her hand. "Even a trip to buy fruit is like a honeymoon with you."

"Well, *almost* like a honeymoon," she giggled, rubbing her nose against his.

"Hey, I got an idea," he grinned as he led her to the cooler's heavy doors. "C'mon."

"What are you doing?"

He ushered her in, checking to see if anyone was watching. "You'll see, Mrs. Molinaro."

The second she stepped into the frigid space, Pauly had his hands on her. He felt her up and steered her against the wire shelves, kissing her like a lovesick teenager under the bleachers.

"Oh, Pauly," she said between kisses, "this rack is so cold against my back."

"But you're so hot," he said, mouth open as he kissed her neck. "And so is *your* rack."

She resisted, sort of, but soon they were necking against a pallet of ice cream.

"Someone will see us," she managed.

"So?"

"So," she said, pulling away, "we should stop. Besides, it's freezing in here."

"Baby," he whined, "you ruin my fun."

"Come on, ya big lug," she said, "let's get out of here."

He stepped around her to open the door, but it was futile. He tried again, and a third time. The door failed to budge. Millie rubbed her shoulders.

"Come on," she said, "it's cold."

"I'm trying," Pauly said, yanking the door handle. "It won't open."

"What?"

"I think we're locked in here," he said, rattling the door but to no avail.

Then the lights went out and they saw the garage-style door rolling closed, darkening the space from top to bottom.

"Pauly! What are we going to do? It's freezing in here!"

He shook the door handle again. No luck. "Baby, you got your tools with you?"

"The lock's on the outside, genius. Nothing to pick from the inside."

"Madonn'," Pauly said, the gravity of the situation settling in. He fumbled for his phone in the dark, but it fell from his pocket. "You got your phone?"

"In the car," Millie said, shivering. "Why did she leave? Didn't she know we were here?"

"Maybe she thought we left," Pauly said. "But you'd think she'd see our car in the lot."

Millie pushed against Pauly, trying to warm up. "It's so cold."

"This ain't the worst thing that could happen," he quipped. "We *are* finally alone."

She smacked his chest. "Will you stop? We'll freeze to death if we stay in here."

"All the more reason to build up some body heat," he said playfully.

"Pauly! I'm serious. We need to find a way out of here. Come on, think."

He ran his hands through his hair, realizing it might be time to panic. Then, a bright blue light came from the floor, followed by a buzz. He looked over to see his phone.

INCOMING CALL

He fumbled toward it, smacking his shin on a wooden pallet. The light was dim, but he followed it until he got close enough to see a photo of Dom dressed in a tuxedo jacket and holding a pina colada, taken on their wedding day. Pauly dropped to his knees on the cement floor, groaning, and reached for the phone. But before he could get his hand on it, it went silent.

"Oh, gimme a friggin' break," he said, his knees shaking on the cold floor. "Come on, Dominic. Call me back." He held onto the frigid shelving unit and turned his head, reaching as far as he could beneath it. Then his phone lit up again.

NEW VOICEMAIL FROM DOM PANICIO.

The light remained just long enough for Pauly to locate the phone and grab it. Without even listening to the message, he dialed Dom's number. But it wouldn't connect.

"Madonn'," he said, "I can't believe it. No service in here."

"Give me that," Millie said, taking the phone from his hands.

"What are you doing?"

"Calling 911," she said. "It should still connect."

"We can't call 911," he said, pulling the phone from her hand.

"We can, and we will," she said, taking it back again.

"Baby," he cautioned, "you know what Dom and I used to do for a living, right?"

"You think anyone out here knows what you used to do for a living? I'm freezing my caboose off. We're getting out of here." She began to dial but he snatched it away.

"Baby, baby, no," he said. "I know you're new to this life, but that's a risk we don't take. We can find another way out of here."

Her teeth were chattering now. "All right, but hurry up," she said. "These shorts and sandals aren't going to keep me warm much longer."

Using a flashlight app, he held up his phone and scanned the cooler for an escape route. "Gotta be another door, right?"

Millie rubbed her hands over her arms to fight off the chill. "Maybe an alarm?"

"Alarms bring cops, baby," he reminded. "Can't do that." He looked around, still seeing no way to escape. Then his phone rang again. He answered it but the signal was weak. "Dom!"

"I got … news … Dion." Then his voice cut out. By the time Pauly could hear him again, Dom said, "Where you at? Geez, this connection is terrible."

"Me and Millie are trapped in the cooler at the farm stand," he said.

"Your filly crapped a boozer in the farmland? What are you talking about? Did your wife take you to that wine bar the girls went to the other day?"

"No, listen," Pauly implored, "we're TRAPPED in the COOLER at the FARM STAND."

"Now, see, that makes no sense, either. Why would the farm stand have a cooler?"

"For the ice crea—DOM! We need help. The girl working here left and we're locked in. Millie's gonna freeze."

"Holy cannoli," Dom said, "that's some shit. What farm stand?"

"The one by the freeway onramp," Pauly explained.

"We'll be right there … oh, shit. No, we won't. You got the car."

Pauly closed his eyes. "Shit."

"Get an Uber!" Pauly heard one of the triplets yell in the background.

"Uber! Right!" Dom said. "Hang on, Pauly. We'll be there as soon as we can. And did you hear what I said about Dion? He's been—"

But the call dropped. Pauly hung up and used the phone's flashlight again to locate Millie. Then he wrapped himself around her, rubbing her bare arms to keep her warm. "Don't worry, baby. They're on their way."

"Why?"

"Because Dom's my best friend," Pauly said.

"No, I mean why would someone lock us in here?"

"You think they did it on purpose?"

"Maybe not for us, but for someone else," she said.

Pauly tilted his head. "What do you mean?"

"For someone who's not 'new to this life,' you sure can be thick sometimes," she said. "Remember when we got out of the car? That truck was in a real hurry."

Pauly thought for a moment. "Yeah, all right …"

"Doesn't that seem odd? Who's in a hurry to get away from a farm stand?"

"Hm, I think you have a point," he said.

"And, the girl said that one of the Maggiolis usually stocks the cooler around now. Usually the grandson, isn't that what she said?"

"You don't think—"

"That those guys sabotaged the door, expecting to trap him inside here? You're damn right I do. First the kid disappears and now this? Seems a little suspicious."

"Yeah, and Dom said they got some news about him. Maybe he's been found?"

Millie was shaking uncontrollably by now. "We need to be found. Soon."

* * *

Across town, Chavonne Occhipinti put her credit card back in her wallet and gathered her shopping bags full of beauty products from Vista Verde's spa. With a flounce of her chestnut hair, she pulled on her dark sunglasses and stepped into the late evening sunshine. The air was thick with the scent of garlic as she waited for the valet.

"Here you go, Miss Occhipinti," he said, curbing her gleaming new roadster. "I see you got yourself something nice and sporty."

She faked a smile and pushed past him, then moved the seat up to fit her more petite frame. "It was time for something new," she said, placing her bags in the passenger seat.

"So, you got plans tonight?" the valet asked, full of hope.

She revved the engine. "I do," she said, handing him a $50 bill before she roared off.

The valet watched the roadster wind down the road, his acne-dotted face draped in awe.

"Keith!"

He turned to see another attendant, Wyatt, running toward him.

"Was that Chavonne Occhipinti?"

The valet nodded. "Yeah, why?"

Wyatt, nearly breathless, came to a stop as sirens began to ring out. "That is one lucky lady," he said. "Not five minutes after she finished her massage, the room caught on fire."

"What? What happened?"

"Candles fell over," Wyatt explained. "Whole room went up."

A fire truck pulled up. As Wyatt directed it toward the spa, Keith asked, "Anyone hurt?"

Wyatt shook his head. "No, but it looks like she got out of there just in time."

A slim woman with a limp emerged from the country club and let out an impatient sigh. Keith's head jerked around. "Good evening, Mrs. Maggioli. Is Mr. Maggioli with you?"

"He's away on business," Gloria Maggioli said, barely looking up from her fresh manicure.

"I see," Keith replied. "I'll get your car right away."

* * *

"What took you so long?" Pauly asked through the wall where Dom was banging his fist.

"Waiting for Uber to arrive," Dom said. "But we're here now. I'm gonna go to the front and see if we can pry open the roll-up door. Hang tight."

Pauly wrapped his arms tighter around Millie. "You hear that, baby? We'll be out soon."

"Millie," Susan yelled from outside, "you doin' okay?"

"F-f-freezing," Millie said.

"It won't be long," Margaret said. "We're gonna help Dom. Don't worry."

Millie's teeth chattered uncontrollably. But soon the heavy door creaked, and a dim light dawned throughout the space. Dom ran to the cooler and tried the door.

Locked.

He looked around. "Might have to break this glass," he said.

"That'll bring the cops," Millie said, putting a smile on Pauly's face. "Mags, get my purse out of the rental car and use my lock pick set."

Pauly's smile turned to an expression of confusion.

"What?" Millie said. "I'm not the only can opener in this family."

Minutes later, Margaret disabled the lock. When Dom swung the door open, a business card fell from the jamb. Susan snatched off the ground and stuffed it in her pocket, not wanting to waste time. Pauly pushed Millie out of the cooler and all five hurried out of the farm stand. While Margaret started the car and got the heater going, Dom and Pauly managed to close the roll-up door. Susan threw a blanket from the trunk around Millie. The men got in the car and Dom turned on the parking lights so he could ease through the dirt lot and onto the empty road.

"Well, this is interesting," Susan said, looking at the business card.

"Is that what was stuck in the door?" Dom asked from the driver's seat.

"Yeah," Susan said, reading the card aloud. "Occhipinti Vineyards."

"Huh," Pauly mused. "Oh, you said you had news about Dion. What is it?"

Dom steered the sedan onto Bel Monte Boulevard, just making the light. "He's dead."

| 10 |

Dom finished his wine and got up from the dining table, leaving Pauly, Millie, Margaret, and Susan to think about the grim news he'd just given them.

"And you're absolutely sure?" Pauly asked, as if hoping it wasn't true.

Margaret refilled the wine glasses and Susan picked at a piece of sourdough bread.

"Coroner reports don't lie," Dom said. "While you were out, Susan got into the coroner's database. They processed a twenty-six-year-old two weeks ago. Fits Dion's description."

"Good job, Susie," Millie said.

Susan shrugged. "Remember when I dated that college whiz kid?"

"That was five years ago," Margaret piped up. "Forty-year age gap. Who could forget?"

"It was thirty-three years, and he obviously appreciated the finer things in life," Susan said. "Anyway, he taught me that you can find anything if you know where to look."

"Bet you taught him a few things," Margaret mused, then sipped her wine.

"But how are you sure that it's Dion?" Pauly asked.

"The church had a closed service for a member of the Maggioli family shortly afterward," Susan replied. "And a space was created at the Maggioli family crypt very recently. As the oldest cemetery here in town, there are already spaces reserved for the elder members of the family. So, if they had to create a new space, that would mean someone died unexpectedly."

"So, the family knows he's dead?" Millie asked.

"Yep," Dom confirmed, "but for some reason, they're keeping it quiet."

Margaret picked up the newspaper. "And this is interesting," she said, pointing to an article on the front page.

LAND SOLD TO MYSTERY BUYER

By Kate Kendall

She read aloud, "A controversial land transaction has been completed, according to a City official who spoke on condition of anonymity, but the buyer's identity has been shielded. The sixty-acre parcel, nestled between property owned by Occhipinti Vineyards and Maggioli Garlic Growers, has been highly desirable since it was first listed for sale two years ago, after the original owner filed bankruptcy. A purchase price was not given, but it is expected to be one of the most valuable pieces of property in South County."

"What is it with those two families?" Millie wondered aloud.

Dom shook his head. "I dunno, but I got a bad feeling."

"Have you told Florence yet?" Pauly asked.

"Nah, we just figured it out when you called," he said. "It's late there. I'll let her sleep and call in the morning. I hate knowin' I'm gonna break her heart. Hopefully, she takes my call."

The silence that accompanies churning thoughts of life's unpleasantries filled the room.

"Anyway," Dom said, "I'm goin' to bed. Goodnight."

"Goodnight," the others chorused.

Pauly watched him disappear up the stairs and waited until he heard the bedroom door close. He looked at Millie and squeezed her hand. "He's still so madly in love with her," he said.

* * *

Dom rolled over and checked the clock. Barely 5:30 a.m. But that would be 8:30 on the east coast. Florence liked to be up early. She'd probably be on her fourth cigarette by now, taking a break with another cup of coffee after tidying up the house. He reached for his phone.

FLORENCE, I HAVE SOME NEW—

He deleted that and started again.

GOOD MORNING.

He watched the screen, waiting for a reply. Minutes later, it came.

DOM, DO YOU HAVE ANY NEWS?

Unsure of how to break it to her, he typed.

YES. CAN I CALL YOU? EASIER THAN TYPING.

NO CALL, came the immediate reply. CAN'T TALK. JUST TYPE.

A frown clouded his face. He didn't want to do this over a screen.

OK, I'LL TYPE A LITTLE, SEND SO YOU CAN READ, THEN TYPE SOME MORE.

SOUNDS GOOD.

Dom thought about how to compose the message. Better to just start with the truth.

I'M SORRY TO TELL YOU THAT DION IS...

His stomach clenched, thinking about how much this was going to hurt Florence.

DEAD. I DON'T HAVE DETAILS YET. WE JUST KNOW THAT HE DIED AND HIS FAMILY IS KEEPING IT QUIET.

He waited for her to answer.

OH GOD, NO.

He pictured her, in her pastel housecoat, crumbling into a heap on her saggy sofa. All he wanted was to comfort her, pull her close and let her sob. But she had a new husband now. And more than anything, he wanted her to be happy. Even if that meant another man comforting her.

FLO, I'M REALLY SORRY. THIS IS WHY I WANTED TO CALL YOU.

NO, I CAN'T TALK. HOW DID IT HAPPEN? WAS IT AN ACCIDENT?

Dom imagined her husband, WhateverHisNameWas, walking into the living room, seeing her crying, and embracing her. His fingers trembled as he typed the next lines.

TOO SOON TO TELL BUT WE'RE WORKING ON IT. PAULY'S SISTER-IN-LAW, SUSAN, SAW THE CORONER'S REPORT. LOOKS LIKE HE DIED FROM BLUNT FORCE TRAUMA. HE WAS FOUND FACE DOWN UNDER A TREE. COULD BE AN ACCIDENT.

Before she could reply, he typed more.

NOT GONNA LIE, SOMETHING IS VERY WEIRD ABOUT THIS WHOLE THING.

Then it came.

WAS IT CARLO?

Dom's eyes widened at the boldness of her accusation.

DON'T KNOW. THAT WHOLE FAMILY SEEMS... SHADY.

Florence typed back, BUT NOT GLORIA. I'LL NEVER UNDERSTAND WHY SHE GOT MIXED UP WITH HIM. I DON'T THINK THEIR MARRIAGE WAS HAPPY. SOMETHING BAD HAPPENED YEARS AGO. SURPRISED SHE DIDN'T LEAVE.

Dom scratched his head. OH? ANY IDEA WHAT IT WAS?

NO. SHE WOULDN'T TELL ME. BUT DION WAS JUST A BABY. AND I THINK THAT'S WHY SHE STAYED. I WISH I COULD'VE TALKED HER INTO LEAVING AND STAYING WITH US. BUT OUR LIFE WASN'T VERY STABLE, YOU KNOW?

His heart sank, crushed to think about all the trouble he'd put her through. All those years. Always looking over their shoulders. Never knowing if he was walking into a hit. The worry and paranoia that stayed with them 24/7. No wonder she left.

I KNOW. FLO, I WANT YOU TO KNOW HOW SORRY I AM FOR ALL THAT.

This would be easier if she'd talk to him. He got up his nerve, then typed, BUT YOU'RE WITH A MAN WHO TAKES BETTER CARE OF YOU NOW. YOU DESERVE THAT.

He could see the bubbles that indicated she was typing, but nothing came. Dom got up and looked out the window. The early light reflected from the roof next door. On the sidewalk, a quartet of old men in fedoras shuffled along. When his phone buzzed, her reply was so unexpected he read it twice.

ACTUALLY, I'M ALL ALONE. I HAVEN'T TOLD YOU THIS, BUT RAFAEL PASSED AWAY A FEW MONTHS AGO. HAD A HEART ATTACK AT THE BREAKFAST TABLE. FELL RIGHT INTO HIS CAFÉ BUSTELO. NEVER MADE IT TO THE HOSPITAL. JUST LIKE THAT, HE WAS GONE.

Dom was aghast. Rattled that she was going through two awful things at once and that he couldn't be there for her. Instinctively, he dialed her number. But it just rang.

I TOLD YOU. DON'T CALL, she texted a minute after Dom hung up. I CAN'T TALK.

This was unlike her, Dom thought. Unless she thought her phone might be bugged?

CAN'T OR WON'T?

Nervously, he waited for her answer.

CAN'T. LEAVE IT AT THAT.

Confused, Dom slipped back into the paranoid mode of second guesses that had overshadowed his life when he was with her. If her phone were bugged, she might be at a greater risk than he realized. Maybe someone knew she'd sent him to check on Dion. And between what happened to him, and his family's reputation, Dom's uneasiness quickly evolved into panic.

OK, he typed, his stomach roiling. LISTEN, YOU NEED ANYTHING, YOU LET ME KNOW. DAY OR NIGHT, DOESN'T MATTER. I STILL GOT CONNECTIONS THERE.

THOUGHT YOU WERE OUT OF THAT LIFE, Florence replied.

Dom's words sunk in as he watched them appear on the screen. NO ONE'S EVER OUT OF THAT LIFE.

He hit send, thinking about who he might trust to check on Flo if it became necessary. After the last job with Pauly in Seattle, he'd made a clean break. Cut off every connection he could and walked away. But there had to be somebody.

I'LL BE FINE. PLEASE LET ME KNOW WHAT YOU FIND OUT.

WILL DO.

GOTTA GO. AND DOM, she typed, THANKS FOR DOING THIS. IT MEANS A LOT.

There were a million things to say. But more than ever, he wanted to hear her voice.

ANYTHING FOR YOU.

He watched the screen, eagerly waiting. But no answer came. Finally, he set his phone on the nightstand. Then he pulled up the covers and tried to get back to sleep.

* * *

By 6:30, he was still wide awake, so he quietly got dressed and wrote out a note.

Couldn't sleep. Going out for a coffee. I'll bring back some donuts. See you mugs later.

He pulled on a windbreaker and tied his shoes. Then he descended the steps of the old Victorian, noting the smell of garlic in the misty air. It was only two blocks to the downtown corridor and the walk was pleasant. Cool with a gentle breeze. An occasional car shushed by, but mostly Dom heard chittering birds and his own sneaker-clad footfalls on the pavement. As he approached Central Road, he could smell freshly brewed coffee. He was longing for an espresso and instinctively followed the scent until he was inside the café at the corner. Taking his place in line, he looked around. Dark wood lined the lower half of the walls, a rich mocha-tinted paint above. Old burlap coffee sacks were tacked up alongside postcards from around the globe. Overhead was a large mural showing a world map, with various coffee-growing regions highlighted. In the back, the four old men in fedoras sipped espresso and read newspapers.

Dom smiled, recalling a variation of this scene replaying numerous times in his old neighborhood. *Gli uomini anziani,* or the old men, as they were called. Retired after a good life of hard work, many widowed, gathering with their counterparts to socialize and do the things they wouldn't normally do if they were alone. It was part of the collective experience that comes with growing up in this lifestyle. Regardless of how they'd spent their years, the elders always commanded respect in their community.

"Can I help you?"

Dom turned to the young lady at the counter. *"Un espresso doppio, per favore,"* he said, inspired by the sight of the old men and lapsing into the language of his grandparents.

"Here or to go?"

He eyed the table, tempted to join the men. But on second thought, he didn't want to intrude. Besides, he still had to buy donuts.

"To go," he said.

She directed him to the register near the back table. As he paid for his espresso, he strained to overhear their conversation.

"You see that gal at the wine bar the other day?" the big one said behind his *Town Crier.*

"We all saw her, Lucky," another said. "We were there. They talked to us. We talked to them. We saw."

"I think she likes me," the big one said.

"You see this story about the land sale?" a third one asked. Two of them sipped their espresso in silence. "I wonder who bought that."

"I hope it was someone local," another said. "Hate to see this town turned over by big corporations. Those hotshots from Silicon Valley want to make this their playground and ruin what's been built here."

"I think she likes me," the big one said to no one in particular, "because she smiled. Did you see that smile?"

The first man moved his newspaper to the side and stared directly at the big one, a look of disgust on his face. Then he spread out the paper again and went back to reading.

"Your espresso," called the barista.

Dom spun toward the counter and picked up his order. *"Grazie,"* he said, raising his voice as if hoping to be overheard. Then he turned back to the table. The man facing him was raising his cup to take a sip. Dom tilted his cup as if making a toast. The man nodded, toasting in response, and Dom walked away.

"And triplets," the big one said, "can you believe that?"

"Lucky," the first man said, rattling his newspaper.

Then the others chimed in, "Shut up."

Dom stepped onto the sidewalk and looked up and down Central Road. He knew he'd seen a donut shop around here somewhere. Again, he let his nose do the navigating and soon he was passing a bridal shope and a vacuum repair before coming to a stop in front of a bakery.

OPEN 7 AM DAILY, read the sign on the front door, UNTIL WE'RE SOLD OUT.

Dom checked his watch. Five more minutes. He sipped his espresso and thought about Florence. How many nights had they sat at a restaurant, talking about their dreams while nursing their coffee and nibbling cannoli? He liked his double shot. "Dark and strong, just like you," she used to tease. Meanwhile, Florence preferred a cappuccino, dusted with cinnamon. "And that's light and frothy, just like you," Dom would counter. Their banter never got old.

As the bakery door swung open, a tall, white-aproned man said, "Good morning."

Dom entered the shop and was overwhelmed by the sweet aromas.

"Good morning," he said. "It smells fantastic in here. I'm gonna get a dozen."

The man assembled a pink box and waited for Dom's selections. Leaning over, Dom studied the case, inspecting maple crullers and glazed old-fashioneds as the shop's door opened.

"Good morning, Mrs. Rosetto," the donut man said. "Be with you in a minute."

Dom wondered if Susan or Margaret would prefer a cinnamon roll. He rubbed his belly, still sore from the ostrich farm incident. Patiently, the man waited with the empty box.

"All right," Dom finally said, "how about two chocolate iced, two glazed old-fashioned, two chocolate crullers, two maple bars … how many is that?"

"Eight," the man said. "You got four more."

"All right," Dom said, "gimme two cinnamon rolls, and … ah, I can't decide."

"Try the apple fritters," said the woman behind him. "They're fabulous."

Dom straightened up and turned around to see a petite woman with graying hair. She wore a neat navy sheath dress, with navy and cream spectator pumps and a matching hat. A sapphire and pearl pin protruded from the side. Dom was suddenly aware that he'd been leaning over, most indelicately, in front of her. His face reddened. "Oh, apple fritters, you say?"

She smiled. "Trust me. Best in all of South County."

Dom turned to the man at the counter. "You heard the lady. Two apple fritters, please."

When Dom pulled out his debit card, the man said, "Sorry, we only take cash."

"Oh, I didn't realize—" Dom said, reaching into his wallet. But it was empty except for a few singles. "I'm just visiting here. Madonn'… I don't seem to have any—"

"Will you allow me to pay for that?" the woman behind him asked, stepping forward.

"Oh, ma'am, I can't—"

"Nonsense," she said, "it'll be my pleasure." She pulled a $20 out of her navy clutch and handed it to the man at the counter.

"I don't know how I'd repay you, Mrs., uh—"

"Rosetto," she said. "You can repay me by doing a good deed for someone else."

"I promise," Dom said, taking the box.

She smiled. "I hope you enjoy your visit. And your apple fritters."

"Mrs. Rosetto," he said, "thank you again. I'm sure we will."

He felt even more awkward than before, letting a woman pay for his donuts. So, he thanked her one more time and made his way to the door. The men in the fedoras were standing in front of the coffee shop, arguing about something, if Dom guessed correctly. He stopped at the next storefront, an antique shop, and looked in the window. His head turned when Mrs. Rosetto emerged from the donut shop, carrying two pink boxes. Her shapely figure swished to the passenger side of a classic Mercedes, where she leaned over and put the boxes on the seat.

Madonn'. That bakery dame's got some dough.

He thought about what he'd given up by getting out of his old lifestyle. That heist in Seattle had paid off, but he wondered if it would be enough to live on, however long he had left. Mrs. Rosetto's Mercedes started up and he watched her make a U-turn and drive off. His espresso warmed him as he walked the few blocks back to the Victorian. He huffed up the steps. Years of carrying extra weight hadn't been kind to his joints and his knees were always achy these days. He set his coffee and the donut box on the café table on the porch so he could retrieve his key. As he pulled the screen open, a piece of paper fell to the welcome mat.

OCCHIPINTI HARVEST GALA
JOIN US FOR THE FUNDRAISER OF THE YEAR
RAFFLE * AUCTION * DOOR PRIZES
HELP SUPPORT YOUR COMMUNITY
THIS SATURDAY

Well, let's see what these schmoes have to say for themselves.

| 11 |

"After you, ladies," Dom said, waiting by the car with Pauly. "You'll melt in this heat."

Susan, Margaret, and Millie trod up the path to the winery's ornate grounds. Occhipinti Vineyards was as decadent as Dom had imagined. Lush green lawns, graceful Mediterranean touches, and rows of vineyards as far as he could see. It felt massive yet quaint all at once.

A curly-haired young man in a burgundy suit approached. "Here, kid," Dom said, handing over his keys and reaching into his wallet. A blank stare followed. "Sorry. Thought you was the val-et."

"No," the muscular man chuckled. "But that's a nice ride you got."

"Thanks," Dom said, his stomach tightening.

"Great accent. New York?"

"Born and raised," Pauly said.

"Yeah, Staten Island," Dom clarified.

"Oh, I could tell. Somethin' about you. In fact, you seem like the kinda guys I need."

"For what?" Pauly asked.

The man looked around the parking lot. "You wanna do a job? Make some money?"

"What kinda job?" Dom asked.

The man waved off the female valet who was hurrying over to the rental car. When she turned, the man said, "Security. Unless you're more into transportation. Up to you."

Dom and Pauly exchanged a glance.

"Pays thirty large," the man said, "each. More if you want it."

Dom reckoned thirty grand would ease some burdens. "Can we think about it?" he asked.

The man slapped him on the back. "Sure, sure," he said. "You just let me know."

"How do we get in touch?" Dom asked.

The man shook their hands, gave Pauly a card, and said, "Name's Onorato." Then he left.

"Huh," Pauly said. "Look familiar?"

He held the card up for Dom, who read it aloud.

"You don't suppose?"

* * *

Rialta Occhipinti looked over the gala's seating chart. "Chavonne!" she barked.

Her daughter tried to hide a grimace as she looked up from a cluster of friends. "Yes?"

"Come here," Rialta said, "now."

She walked over, stopping briefly to shake hands with the four older men in fedoras at a nearby table. Rialta didn't even let her speak.

"Why are the Maggiolis so far from the dais?"

"They requested a table for ten," Chavonne replied. "I wasn't even sure they'd show up. But we only do tables of eight and we needed more room for the dais, so we moved—"

"Not acceptable," Rialta waved her hand, dismissing her. "They're in mourning, and we must show solidarity. They should be up front. And why is Onorato D'Agostini at your table?"

"He works for dad and—"

"And he's your ex. Do you know how bad that looks so soon after Dion's death?"

"No one really knew we were dating," Chavonne said, her voice tinged with frustration.

Rialta shot an icy glare. "People at this gala knew," she said, lowering her voice to a stern rebuke. "Enough people knew. Most importantly, the Maggiolis knew. These arrangements will raise questions when we should focus on celebrating the harvest and promoting the family business. We've already lost the greatest PR opportunity, announcing your engagement, with Dion's death. How dare you threaten our reputation with your carelessness, *piccola ragazza*."

Carelessness? PR opportunity? But the worst of it: *Little girl.* That was one of the most condescending things Chavonne's mother could ever call her. And Rialta knew how much her daughter hated it.

"We're about to start seating people," Chavonne said through a forced smile, aware that numerous guests had already arrived. "What do you suggest—"

"I suggest you figure out how to fix this," Rialta snapped, "before your father finds out."

Her green eyes flashed like a lightning bolt striking the earth in the dead of night. Then she turned sharply and extended her long, tawny arm to the elderly gentlemen at a nearby table. *"Signor Zanetti, Signor Volpe, che bello vederti. Signor Tremolada, Signor Giardi, benvenuto."*

Chavonne watched momentarily, resenting her mother's harshness yet admiring her ability to get what she wanted. Like it or not, Rialta was the master to Chavonne's apprentice.

"You all right?" a deep voice behind her said.

She spun to see Onorato, all six feet and five inches of him, draped in a burgundy suit that hugged his broad biceps. A real smile now graced her lips.

"Fine," she said, "but I need to move you to another table."

He looked at Rialta, smiling as she crossed the lavishly decorated patio, greeting guests and receiving compliments on a job well done. His dark brows sunk as he turned to Chavonne.

"Sorry, but it's for the best. And," she said, emboldened, "I need help moving that far table closer to the dais."

"But everything's already set up," he protested. "People are arriving."

"So, let's hurry and get it done," she said, her chestnut mane bouncing as she walked off. He would follow her like a lost puppy, and she knew it. A few months before meeting Dion, she'd broken it off with Onorato, mostly because he wouldn't give her enough space. He'd said that being raised by a single mother had instilled a tendency to nurture women. But his idea of nurturing meant treating her like a fragile flower, incapable of doing anything for herself. Chavonne Occhipinti didn't want to be controlled. But she did know how to translate a man's desires into usefulness. Another valuable lesson from Rialta.

As expected, she turned to see Onorato behind her as she reached the table. She nodded to two waiters. "Help with this," she said, removing two large floral arrangements from the table. She answered their puzzled looks with a succinct, "Right up front. Make room."

Onorato lifted one end of the table while the waiters took the other and nestled it into a tight opening between the other guests. Chavonne set down the centerpieces, then walked away.

"Chavonne," Onorato called after her, "do you have a minute?"

But she was already on to the next task. Moving his place card to a table far from hers.

Nunzio stepped in front of her. "What are you doing?"

She breezed past, not interested in anything he had to say. He grabbed her arm, and she wrenched it away, smiling to mask her anger and hoping no one had seen. "Do not touch me like that," she instructed. "I don't care if you are my brother. I'll flip you on your ass."

"Why did you move Onorato?" he persisted, blocking her again. "He should sit with us."

"Because Mom told me to," she said with satisfaction. "So, if you have a problem with that, ask her. Now get out of my way."

She pushed past him and took a glass of Tempranillo from a server's tray. Retreating to a shady alcove away from the patio, she took a long, slow sip and let the plum and leather flavors float in her mouth before swallowing. It was already warm and if the pre-gala activity was any indication, this was going to be a wretchedly long day and evening. A bead of sweat descended from the nape of her neck, tracing her spine inside her black and lavender floral dress. She watched as the guests continued to arrive, fanning herself and wishing she was elsewhere.

* * *

"Dom," Pauly said as they walked up to the winery, "you serious about taking that job?"

"I dunno," Dom said. "I mean, it's a lotta dough."

"Yeah, but I thought we agreed—"

"We did," Dom snapped, suddenly defensive. "But come on. Two old guys like us, with no real security, and no marketable skills, as they say. We ain't foolin' nobody but ourselves. You think you're gonna keep Florence happy on whatever you made from that last job?"

"Millie," Pauly corrected.

"What?"

"Millie," he repeated. "Not Florence."

Dom felt his shoulders soften. "Yeah, that's what I meant. Millie."

"Look," Pauly said, "I'm not saying no. I'm just saying I want more information."

"About the job and that guy," Dom added.

"Think he made us?" Pauly asked. "Kinda weird he walked up and offered us a job."

"I guess we got that certain look," Dom figured.

Pauly looked around, trying to spot the young man. Something about him seemed familiar. As they approached the winery gate, a petite woman in a chic, wide-brimmed hat secured with a sparkling pin fiddled with her purse's clasp, dropping her keys.

Dom bent to retrieve them. "Allow me," he said. Friction burned his belly as it rubbed his waistband.

"Thank you," she said. "Oh, wait a minute, I recognize you."

He tucked in his butt cheeks as he turned around, embarrassed when he saw her. "Oh, the Apple Fritter Lady! I mean, Mrs. ... I'm sorry, I can't recall."

"Rosetto," she said. "Giuseppina Rosetto. Pleased to make your acquaintance, Mr.?"

"Dom," he said, preferring not to give a last name. "And this is my friend, Pauly."

"Nice to meet you," she said, shaking hands.

"Pauly, Mrs. Rosetto—"

"Giuseppina," she said, "please."

"Giuseppina was kind enough to pay for our donuts the other day," Dom explained. "I didn't know they only took cash and—"

"Giuseppina, *amica*," came a voice inside the gates. "Don't you look lovely?"

"Oh, excuse me," Giuseppina said, waving to a woman with long black hair. "I hope we can catch up inside. Rialta!"

Dom and Pauly watched as the women embraced and exchanged air kisses.

"She's quite the looker," Pauly said. "Uptown broad."

Dom chuckled, "You can say that again."

"Come on," Pauly said, "let's find the girls."

* * *

Chavonne sipped her wine from her hiding place off the patio. Silvestro and Nunzio were positioned around Onorato. Three wide guys and barely a brain cell between them, she observed. Next to them was Giuseppina Rosetta, a widow and longtime patron who was heavily involved in the historical society and local philanthropy efforts. Giuseppina's husband, Antonio, had some dealings with Carlo Maggioli. Gone a few years, Antonio's name was rarely spoken. She chatted with Mathilde and Miguel da Conceicao and Albert Watson, Mayor Denise Watson's husband.

The Hat Pack—that's what everyone called them—sat at the next table. Ottavio Tremolada, Eufrasio Volpe, Bartolomeo Zanetti, and Fortunato Giardi. They went just about everywhere together and were easy to spot with their fedoras. Even in sweltering heat, they'd be dressed to the nines, shirt sleeves buttoned, loafers polished.

A group of two men and three women, all in their late fifties or early sixties, stood at the bar. Chavonne had never seen them before, but she wondered if the women were triplets. Each wore a long, ivory crepe skirt with a pastel sweater. A bit casual for this event, Chavonne noted.

A string quartet played Pachelbel's *Canon in D* as more guests entered. There were city council members, the president of the chamber of commerce, and several business owners. But every head turned when Ignazio Maggioli, dressed in a sharp black suit, led his wife, Adalgisa, into the space. She wore a black chiffon gown that belied her septuagenarian age, and her ears dripped with a pair of simple diamond chandelier earrings. Chavonne started toward them but saw that her father, Lazaro, had already intercepted the couple. Clasping his large hand over Ignazio's, he embraced the older man, then kissed Adalgisa's cheek. Rialta immediately appeared by his side and greeted them in kind before showing them to their table. Just behind them, Lucrezia, Tomasso, and Ysabella Maggioli entered. Hugo and Maria Cardenas and Enzo and Rowena Ferreira came next. Finally, Gloria Maggioli, dressed in a simple black dress and flats, walked slowly across the patio. Lazaro pulled out a chair for her and she sat at the table.

Chavonne took a final sip of her wine, then placed the empty glass on a waiter's tray. "Gloria," she said, coming up behind the frail woman and leaning over to rest her hands on Gloria's shoulders. "How are you?"

Clutching Chavonne's hands, she said, "I'm here. Dion would want that. How are you?"

Chavonne shrugged. "I'm here," she said. "Work keeps me busy."

They exchanged a silent smile, then Chavonne asked. "Isn't Carlo joining you?"

Gloria shook her head. "He's away on business."

Chavonne straightened her shoulders. Now she knew why they'd requested a table for ten. As much as Carlo seemed to despise Lazaro, he always attended the gala. She noticed two waiters standing together, sharing a laugh.

"Well," Chavonne said, "it's good to see you. I hope we can chat later. If you'll excuse me, I need to check on the food service."

She walked toward the kitchen, passing the table with the two men and the triplets.

"If I want anything done right, I have to do it myself," she muttered, glaring at the waiters. She continued toward the kitchen, stopping occasionally to greet various guests. The Occhipinti Vineyards Harvest Gala was the social event of the season. And Daddy had agreed to give her more input in the planning this year. She wanted to make sure everything was perfect. As she stepped into the kitchen, her phone buzzed.

YOU LOOK SAD. I TOLD YOU THE OTHER DAY, EVERYTHING WILL BE FINE.

She looked around, but the patio was packed with guests now. The auction was due to begin any minute and she didn't have time for this. She checked the trays, lined with spring asparagus in puff pastry tartlets, petite caprese skewers, and crostini topped with chevre and figs. A perfect start to this event, she assured herself.

DON'T IGNORE ME, came the next text. But she muted her phone and tucked it into a pocket as she returned to the patio. Her parents stood at the dais and the string quartet cut short their version of Beethoven's *Eine Kleine Nacthmusik*. Lazaro gripped the microphone.

"My friends," he said, "welcome to our annual gala. It's good to see all of you here as we celebrate this year's harvest. I'm pleased to see so many familiar faces and some new ones. The appetizers are arriving, right on time. Everyone, please join me in applauding my lovely daughter, Chavonne, for her excellent work in coordinating the menu for this year's event."

The patio burst into applause. Chavonne bowed in recognition and applauded her father.

"Now," Lazaro continued, "the auction will start soon. We have some wonderful packages that have been put together to raise funds for the city's community center, as well as Sainte Cecelia's safe parking program, which allows families who are unhoused to use RVs that have been donated and are parked on the church property. I hope you'll open your hearts and your wallets to support these worthy causes. I think our fundraising committee has really outdone themselves this year. Be prepared for some incredible surprises."

A buzz traveled through the patio as plates arrived. Chavonne sat next to Nunzio, who greeted her with a cold stare. She exchanged cordial chatter with her tablemates, mostly Occhipinti executives, and sat up straight, knowing her mother's eyes were always on her.

"Let's start the auction, shall we?" Lazaro announced. "I'm going to hand the emcee duties to my brother, Ubaldo, who serves on our executive board."

Chavonne watched her uncle, slimmer and frailer than her father, rise and take the microphone. Kindly and sweet, there was a slowness to Ubaldo that no one in the family ever discussed. Lazaro felt the need care for him, including him in most business ventures.

"Ladies and gentlemen," he began, his words carefully measured, "our first item ... is a wonderful basket from the Maggioli family." He waited for a brief outbreak of applause to die down. He pointed at Ignazio who acknowledged the applause with a wave.

"Now," he said, "can I get someone to show this basket? Chavonne, would you mind?"

She stepped forward. Holding the basket, she walked the length of the patio while Ubaldo described the contents, most of which were represented by photos. One premium crate of garlic. Various jars of chopped, minced, crushed, and pickled garlic, giardiniera, garlic-based pasta sauce, pesto, and roasted garlic. A gourmet roasting set, fine linen kitchen towels, and a family cookbook that included some of the Maggiolis' oldest, most cherished recipes. But the big-ticket item was a subscription to receive free garlic for a year.

"Madonn', that's a lotta garlic," said one of the dark-haired men sitting with the triplets, a little louder than appropriate. Several heads turned to look at him, and the man awkwardly picked up a wine glass and took a sip.

Smiling at Gloria, Chavonne passed the Maggiolis' table. The man with the triplets used a butter knife to cut into his crostini, but instead he sent a chunk of fig onto the patio floor, directly in front of Chavonne. Too late to break her stride, she slid on it, nearly falling into Ignazio's lap. He caught her but the basket tumbled to the ground.

"Oh, I'm so sorry," Chavonne said, righting herself. "Are you all right, Mr. Maggioli?"

Ignazio sat up as the crowd began to murmur. "I'm fine," he said. "Let me help you." He leaned forward in his seat to pick up some of the things that had fallen from the basket. But he stopped when he saw a glinting silver chain.

"How did this get here?" he asked. He snatched it off the floor and held it up.

Chavonne's eyes widened. She'd seen that item before but wouldn't have expected to see it here. Gloria clasped her hand over her mouth, shocked at the sight.

"This is the chain from Dion's St. Christopher medal," Ignazio said, running his warped hand over the broken links of the thick Turkish chain. "I gave it to him for his first communion."

Chavonne's mouth fell open and she tottered on her heels.

"He wore this every day, and I thought it was odd that this wasn't on his body when he was found," Ignazio said, now announcing to everyone that Dion was dead. A stunned, collective gasp fell over the gathering as he stood up. "I don't want to ruin this happy occasion," he said, looking at Lazaro, "but you all should know that Dion died recently. We've tried to keep it private. But our family is heartbroken to have lost such a bright light in our world."

Whispers rumbled through the patio as Chavonne felt her stomach churn. She ran to the kitchen, looking for a sink. An acidic fluid climbed into her esophagus and deposited itself in the basin. As it did, her phone buzzed with another text.

CAREFUL.

| 12 |

"Bro," Silvestro called, "we're going to be late."

Nunzio gave his hair one last combing, then slicked it back with gel. "She can wait," he sniffed. He took a final look in the mirror, sucking in his cheeks and admiring himself.

Silvestro rolled his eyes. "C'mon, pretty boy. We gotta shake down six more customers and make that guy a deadbeat before his loan's due. And find out who bought that land."

"I told you," Nunzio said, "it wasn't Chavonne."

"I'm not so sure about that," Silvestro said, locking their luxury condo at an exclusive golf course enclave. Perched in the hills and mainly populated by middle-aged Boomers who'd made their money in big tech, it seemed like an ill fit for a couple of young executives. Far from the middle of town. Inconvenient when they wanted to go out to the clubs. But the distance made it an ideal place to come home to after a long day of "doing business," as Lazaro called it. No prying eyes here. Folks pulled their Beemers into the garage and closed the door behind them without so much as a wave to their neighbors, so business stayed private.

"Sly, you really think she'd keep that to herself? She *lives* to please Dad. If she'd pulled off that deal, Baby Sister would be dragging us by the balls through a mud puddle of humility."

Silvestro shook his head. "You got an odd way with words, Nunz."

"Maybe, but it's true. She *knows* how much Dad wanted us to close that deal. And she was pissed when he took it out of her hands."

"You're probably right," he said, starting his truck, "but I still don't trust her."

Nunzio laughed. "You think she trusts *us?*"

"She shouldn't," Silvestro chuckled. "I'm just not sure she's figured that out yet."

He roared out of the complex, rattling the windows of other condos. Fifteen minutes later, they met Chavonne at their usual booth in the back of the diner.

"Boys," she said, moving her coffee mug to make room. Silvestro leaned to kiss her cheek, but she scooted the other way as they took seats on either side of her in the curved booth. "Don't," she said.

"And good morning to you," Silvestro said, signaling the waitress for two more coffees.

Chavonne grimaced as they got settled. "I don't have much time today," she said. "So, let's get right to it. Who do you think bought that parcel?"

"I see you're still a girl who can't wait to get what she wants," Nunzio ribbed.

She shot him an icy glance as the coffee arrived, and he sat up straight. Another habit developed from observing Rialta, and Chavonne had perfected it.

Silvestro chimed in, "I don't know. We're hoping you'd have some knowledge to share."

She sipped her coffee slowly, sensing their anticipation in her answer and relishing the fact that it was going unsatisfied. She watched the traffic hum down Central Road as the city slowly came to life. After another sip, she said, "All I know is that it was a cash deal."

Nunzio nearly spit out his coffee. "Cash?"

"Wow," Silvestro said, awed. "You sure?"

Chavonne nodded. "Yep. My IRS source said it was reported the day of the transaction."

"IRS?" Nunzio questioned.

"Any cash transaction over $10,000 is automatically reported by the bank," Chavonne explained. "You really should know that."

"So, we know it was cash," Silvestro said. "What else do we know?"

"Well," Chavonne said, leaning back in the booth, "we know the owner wanted the land to go to a local buyer. Not saying it didn't, but if we assume it stayed in local hands, there aren't many families or businesses who would be able to come up with that much cash."

"How much are we talking?" Nunzio asked, arranging little tubs of creamer in stacks.

"At least $20 million," Chavonne speculated. "The opening bid was around $11 million, but that was obviously low-balled to set up a bidding war. There's no way anyone would've let it go for that price. And again, you really should know this."

Nunzio squirmed and continued to stack the tubs.

"What do you think the odds are that the land went to an outsider?" Silvestro asked.

"Pretty low," Chavonne said. "One of the reasons that property sat idle for so long was that the seller wanted to keep it locally owned. I know they had a fat offer from one of the tech giants up north, hoping to expand their warehouses and move some of their offices down here. Makes sense. Land is cheaper. A lot of people from this area commute to San Jose or farther to tech jobs. Would've been smart. But they were turned down."

"However," Silvestro observed, "that land is just as valuable for agriculture. Growers here would want to block that sale to keep *il terreno fertile* from going to waste."

"Exactly," Chavonne said. "So, I'm confident it was someone local."

"Which means the list of potential buyers is short," Silvestro said.

Nunzio admired the creamer tubs he'd stacked as if he'd erected a cathedral.

"Right," Chavonne said. "So, besides us, who has that kind of money?"

Nunzio looked up. "You're joking, right? Gotta be the Maggiolis."

"Not necessarily," she said. "Dion wanted that land but said he didn't have a deal."

"And you believed him?" Nunzio asked, slapping his hand on the table with enough force to scatter the creamers across the table.

Another icy glare stilled him. "Yes," she said, holding his gaze, "I did. I was hoping he might buy it as a wedding gift, but he said it fell through. And Dion would never lie to me."

Silvestro watched the two of them, impressed with his sister's confidence. It seemed she'd inherited the best negotiating traits from both Rialta and Lazaro. "Okay," he said, "so who else could it be? The da Conceicaos, maybe?"

Chavonne nodded. "Maybe, but I'm not sure why they'd want more property. Seems he was content to retire when the time came. Sold off some smaller holdings a few years ago."

"Right. Maybe the Ortegas?"

"Doesn't seem like a good fit," Chavonne said. "That's a lot of land for berries."

"The Murphy family?" Nunzio guessed, gathering the creamers again.

"Doubt they could shoulder the tax burden," Chavonne said. "Remember that little to-do with the tax commission they had? Bet they're still paying that off."

"So, maybe not a grower," Silvestro mused. "Other businesses? Philanthropists—"

"What about Giuseppina Rosetto?" Nunzio broke in.

"I thought about her," Chavonne said. "Definitely a possibility. But she doesn't need the land. She mostly deals with charities and schools. Not sure what she'd do with that parcel." Her phone buzzed. She checked it and frowned. "Well," she said, "I'm out of ideas for now. You guys have anything to report? How's Dad's new fundraising effort going?"

Nunzio cleared his throat and put the creamers back in the holder. "Ran into a snag."

"Like what?"

Silvestro smiled. "A couple clients are a little ... *shy* about parting with their money, but we're on it. They'll come around soon."

Chavonne knew better than to question that, especially in public.

"I see," she said. "And how is Dad? I haven't talked to him since the gala."

"He and Zio Ubaldo went fishing today," Silvestro said. "I think he just wanted to get away for a bit. When Dion's chain fell out of that basket, he was rattled."

"We all were," Chavonne said. "I still can't believe that happened. Made our family look bad. I'd like to know who put it there."

Silvestro shrugged while Nunzio fiddled with the creamers again.

"Have the cops announced an investigation?" Chavonne asked, aware they hadn't.

"I don't think so, but people are starting to talk," Nunzio observed.

A tense silence elapsed between them, all eyes darting left and right.

"Yeah, well, not much we can do about that," Chavonne finally said. "This town's not that big. People will always see what they want to see."

Silvestro nodded. "I'm sure it'll be all over the paper this week."

"Kate Kendall will have her big scoop," Chavonne mocked, making finger quotes.

Silvestro rolled his eyes. "As usual."

"Anyway, I need to go," Chavonne said, putting a $20 on the table. Silvestro stood to let her out of the booth. "See you guys later."

As she walked off, the waitress returned to refill their cups. "You want any breakfast?"

"A short stack and two orders of bacon," Nunzio said.

"You?" she asked Silvestro.

He shook his head. "Egg white scramble," he said, "with fruit. Thanks, Darlene."

"Sure," she said. "Also, someone's here to see you. Said he'd wait until your sister left."

They looked up to see Onorato D'Agostini carrying a small backpack.

"What's up, meatheads?" he asked as he slid into the booth.

"Any luck with our little problem?" Silvestro asked.

"Well, bro, two things. For one," Onorato said, a sly grin widening across his face, "I might be adding two more to our crew."

Nunzio looked up from the creamers. "Two more? Who?"

"Coupla old school jabronis I met at the gala," Onorato explained. "I got a second cousin in New York who told me about this squad. Used to run with Sal Alimonto, then disappeared. I don't know their whole story, but they don't sound too bright."

"Not like us," Nunzio boasted as the creamers tumbled onto the table again.

"Right," Onorato said. "Anyway, they're … our kind of people, let's say."

"All right," Silvestro said, "what's the other thing?"

Onorato spread open the backpack, which was filled with cash. "I made a withdrawal."

"From?" Silvestro asked.

"Old lady at the dry cleaners," Onorato said. "Easy mark."

"Is that enough?" Nunzio asked.

Silvestro checked to see if anyone could hear. "Hey," he said, "careful."

"Enough to start the party," Onorato said as his phone rang. He checked the caller ID. "More where that came from, and it looks like we're about to get some help."

| 13 |

Dom sipped his espresso in the Victorian's quiet parlor. The sunbeams spilled into the space, warming the wood trim around the doorway, and reflecting against the martini glasses in the built-in cupboard. He liked being up before everyone else. It gave him time to think. About the years he'd wasted doing things he shouldn't have done. Working so hard to get made that he didn't think about the impact he was making. On others and himself. Always with one hand over his gun and one eye over his shoulder. Hypervigilant, the head shrinkers called it now. A perpetual state of alert. But what he'd done to survive had taken an enormous toll.

He knew he could never go back to his old neighborhood. Not that there was much left for him there anymore. Once Eddie was whacked and Sal Alimonto took over the streets and tried to frame him and Pauly, there wasn't much choice but to escape. That little diamond heist in the Pacific Northwest and the resulting misunderstanding at the Benbow Inn's murder mystery weekend had renewed their zest for life. Made Dom feel like he was still good for something. It was a shame about that Yorkie, sure. But Pauly had met Millie there and started a new adventure. And Susan and Margaret were good company. Dom, however, felt restless. Unfulfilled. Like a canvas waiting for an artist to bring him to life.

Florence had provided that fulfillment once. But he'd driven her away with his shady, unstable ways. He didn't blame her. It was a hard life, not meant for everyone. She was a remarkable woman, strong and loyal to a fault. But she deserved better. And now she was alone.

Instinctively, he pulled out his phone and stared at the keypad. But typing out his feelings seemed impersonal. So, he found a stack of paper in a drawer and sat down to write.

***

Pauly crept down the hall as he hung up the phone. Then he slipped the card back in his wallet and opened the bedroom door. Millie let out a soft sigh as he approached. Watching her sleep was an aphrodisiac and he couldn't wait to get back in bed with her. But when he did, his mind was scattered, troubled. It sounded easy enough. Besides, no one really knew them here. That could be as much of an advantage as a disadvantage, but it wasn't like he hadn't been in these situations before. He figured he and Dom could do this quick job, learn what they needed to learn, and get out of town before anyone caught on.

Millie curled up to him. "Where were you?"

"Had to take a piss like a racehorse," he said, nuzzling her neck. "Let's go back to sleep."

***

"*Cara mia,*" Dom wrote, "I've been thinking."

He looked at his words, then wadded up the page and began on a fresh sheet of paper.

"Sweetheart."

No.

"My dear Florence."

No.

He ran a meaty hand over his face and closed his eyes. He couldn't stop thinking about the guy at the gala. Maybe one more job wouldn't be such a bad idea. Build a little more of a nest egg to give him some flexibility. Money could solve a lot of his problems right now.

A garlic-scented breeze wafted in from the windows, rippling the papers. Remembering the task at hand, he tried to think of what he might say if Florence were there.

"Dear Flo," he wrote, imagining her at the other end of the dining table, sipping her cappuccino as the day began. He remembered those chilly mornings in their tiny bungalow, just the two of them, content to enjoy each other's silent company. Sharing the newspaper. She'd pass him the sports section and then go straight to the crossword puzzle. Whoever finished first read the front page. When it would rain, he'd hear the drizzle pattering the roof. She'd start a second batch of hot water for espresso in the French press. They'd cuddle close and just listen, holding each other, and feeling safe. Then he'd hear the wind kick up and a hard spattering of rain would slam against the window. He'd jump, calculating how quickly he could get to his pistol. She would pat her hand on his thigh, and he'd smell the mélange of Enjoli perfume and stale cigarettes in her hair, taking comfort in her calming presence.

"As I'm here trying to find out what happened to Dion," he wrote, "it's caused me to think. He was so young, had his whole life ahead of him. It seems everyone loved him. It's hard to understand why someone would want to harm him. But as you and I well know, everyone has enemies. We're all the villain in someone else's story."

He looked out the window, eyeing the wispy fog hugging the foothills. Little rivulets of clouds pulling apart like cotton candy against the tree-green landscape.

"I guess what I'm trying to say is that I know I've been that villain for many people. Don't get me wrong. I know some of those guys deserved what they got. I was doing my job and that came with consequences I can't change. But I've been that villain especially for you. And it pains me to say that, but at the time, I thought I was doing what was expected of me. I did what I did because I wanted to succeed. I wanted to provide for you. Make our lives better. It seems so stupid now. Especially because it had the exact opposite effect.

"The things I did put you at risk and made you unhappy. I know that. I should have been a better husband. A better man. And I want you to know how sorry I am. I can't take back what I did. I can't fix the mistakes I made. Mistakes that cost you your peace of mind. Mistakes that cost me the one thing I should have valued over everything else: our marriage.

"Florence, I don't expect you to forgive me, but seeing what happened to Dion has made me realize how short and precious life is. If there's any chance for me to come back into your life, I'd like to try. I promise I will spend whatever time we have left doing what I should have done from the start.

"Loving you. Cherishing you. And taking care of you."

He sat back and read it a few times, unsure of how to end it and struggling to find the right words. To complicate things, he remained conflicted over the potential job. No amount of money would change what he'd done. But another payday might help him make things right with Florence. Noise from the kitchen tore him from his thoughts.

"Good morning," Susan said, walking into the parlor with coffee. "You're up early."

Dom gathered the papers. "Yeah, I couldn't sleep," he bluffed. It wasn't entirely true. He'd been awake early every day, hoping to get a text from Florence.

"Whatcha writing?" Susan asked as she sat down across the table from him.

Deliberately, he creased the papers. "A letter to Florence."

"Don't let me stop you," Susan said. "I didn't mean to interrupt."

"Nah, I'm done for now. I'll finish it later. Ran out of things to say."

Susan sipped her coffee, clearly not buying it.

"So," Dom said, eager to change the subject. "What's everyone doing today?"

Thankfully, Susan took the hint. "Not sure. I want to see if there are any updates to that coroner's report. And Margaret wants to walk up to the library to buy a newspaper. I can't believe this town only publishes a paper once a week."

"Kinda quaint, though. Not much happens here. That paper probably has a small budget."

"I guess," Susan pondered. "But I'm wondering what they'll publish about the gala."

"Good point," Dom said. "How about the newlyweds?"

Susan made a face. "Oh, they've been complaining about not having any privacy."

"Really? Madonn', it's not like we can't hear them every night—"

Susan shuddered. "Cripes, don't remind me. At least your room's farther down the hall. Anyway, I think they said something about a romantic getaway. Whatever that means."

"Well, last time they did get locked in a freezer," Dom recalled.

"Yeah, you'd think that might've cooled them off," Susan countered.

Dom erupted in laughter. He realized it was the first time he'd really laughed in days. Then he thought about Florence and his mood dampened. "Well," he said, gathering his things, "I'm gonna shower. Thanks for making me laugh, Susie."

She hoisted her coffee cup in a salute. "One of my many skills."

Dom hurried past Pauly and Millie's room. Was that moaning he heard? In his room, he set the letter on his nightstand. He thought about reading it one more time but decided to wait until after his shower. His head was as thick with memories as the garlicky aroma that hung over this town like a security blanket. That shower was going to feel good.

| 14 |

Pauly braced against the headboard as Millie rolled off him. With his chest heaving, he wondered if he'd have the stamina to keep up with her. The first few months of marriage had been exciting, but she sure had a lot of energy. He worried that he couldn't satisfy her.

"So," she said, snuggling into his chest hair, "what should we do today?"

Good lord, woman, how about a nap?

Pauly dashed away the thought, trying to come up with a way to spoil her.

"I have a surprise in mind," he said.

"Ooh," she cooed, running her fingers over his hairy chest. "A surprise. What is it?"

He kissed her forehead. "Baby, if I told you, it wouldn't be a surprise. Why don't we—"

A knock at the door interrupted him.

"Hey, you guys ever getting out of that bed?" Margaret asked.

"Madonn'," Pauly groaned as Millie pulled the sheets to her bare shoulders.

"Geez, Mags, can't we have some privacy?"

"Wondering if you're getting a shower," Margaret said. "Susie's done. I want my turn."

"Well," Pauly said to Millie, "that *was* thoughtful of her."

Millie rolled her eyes. "She's the youngest. She's just doing it to mess with me."

"Go ahead," Millie called, slipping her hand under the covers. "We're busy."

Gingerly, he intercepted her. "Baby," he said, "let's save something for later."

She stretched up and kissed his cheek. "You spoil my fun."

"Well, I'm going to spoil you today, Kitten," he said, nuzzling her nose.

She arched her back. "Ooh, I love it when you call me that," she practically purred.

Maybe a few smooches wouldn't wear him out.

* * *

Susan studied her laptop, reading glasses perched on her nose. Meanwhile, Margaret laced up her shoes.

"Find anything yet?" Margaret asked.

Susan tapped a few keys. "It's been updated, but I'm not sure what changed. I wish I'd thought to print the original report," she said. "It'll take forever to read this medical jargon."

"You ready?" Dom asked from the parlor.

Margaret stood. "Yep," she said. "Thanks for going to the library with me."

"Fresh air will do me good," Dom said. He gently patted his thick stomach, remembering the burn. And the apple fritters he'd been eating the past few days. "Besides, I need exercise."

With eyes cartoonishly magnified, Susan looked over her glasses. "You're gonna leave me here with Mr. and Mrs. Fuck Bunny?"

"Put on some music and drown 'em out," Margaret said with a laugh. "Church hymns?"

"There's a broom in the hall closet," Dom offered. "Maybe bang it on the wall?"

"Ugh, don't say bang," Susan said, shaking her head and dismissing them with a wave. "Have fun at the library, kids. Don't get thrown out for whispering too loud."

They laughed as they walked out the front door. Susan watched them descend the steps, noting how good it was to see Dom smile. Then she turned back to her screen.

"Left semicapitis muscle contusion," she read aloud, scratching on her notepad. "Diffuse axonal injury caused by concussive force to the junction of the medulla and spinal cord."

She leaned forward and read it again.

"Semicapitis ... junction of the ... medulla and ... spinal cord." She ran her fingers down the base of her skull, then took off her glasses. "Huh."

* * *

Pauly held the door for Millie as they entered the restaurant. Set in the old city hall building, it featured grand arches, a large, tiled bar, and dozens of tables. The light from the floor to ceiling windows cast a soft glow around the dining room. As the hostess showed them to a table, Pauly pulled out Millie's chair and made sure she was seated comfortably.

"Can I start you with something from the bar?" the hostess asked.

"A glass of red wine sounds good," Pauly said. "What do you suggest?"

The hostess reeled off a short list of selections, but emphasized, "The Occhipinti private reserve cabernet sauvignon is excellent. Shall I bring you a bottle?"

Pauly tried not to flinch. "Two glasses, please."

"Of course," she said before excusing herself.

"We had that Occhipinti wine the other day when the girls and I—" Millie began. Then she paused as she noticed four men in fedoras approaching the front door.

"What?" Pauly asked, turning to look.

"I think we saw those same guys at the wine bar," she said.

Pauly looked carefully. "Weren't they at the gala, too?"

A server delivered their wine.

"Oh, you're right," she said, watching them file out the door. "The big one hit on Susan."

"Really?"

Millie laughed. "Quite the charmer. He said his friends call him Lucky. Maggie and I joked on the way home that she coulda got lucky if it weren't for us third and fourth wheels."

The pair laughed just a shade too loud for the cavernous space. As heads turned, Pauly withdrew, but Millie just sipped her wine.

"Let 'em stare," she shrugged. "I'm out with my sexy husband and we're enjoying some alone time. Who cares what anyone thinks?"

He squeezed her hand. "That's right, Kitten."

"Hey, I need to visit the little girls' room," she said.

"Come to think of it, I gotta hit the can, too," Pauly said.

They asked a server for directions. "Right over there," she said. "Just past the jail cells."

Pauly's face blanched. *"Jail cells?"*

"This building used to house the jail," the server said. "That's where the restrooms are."

"Oh, I love it," Millie squealed. "Pauly, what a great surprise."

"Madonn'," he said, shaking his head as they walked toward the hallway lined with old photos. Sure enough, the letters over the doorway read JAIL.

Two steps into the restroom, he paused. Iron bars guarded the front of the toilet. "Now I've seen everything," he muttered, dashing away unpleasant memories. After hurriedly doing his business, he stepped back into the restaurant. As he waited for Millie, he caught a glimpse of the four men in fedoras, chatting at the curb in front of the restaurant.

"Does the men's room have jail cell doors, too?" she asked, clutching his arm.

"Yeah," he said. "Weird."

"Oh, I think it's a hoot! I bet it would've been too expensive to tear out when they renovated so they just left them there," she said. "Gives the place character."

"Baby, you ever been in jail, for real?"

Millie sipped her wine. "You know the girls and I have been around. But no jail."

"It ain't a pretty place," Pauly said, speaking from the experience of not being lucky enough to wiggle out of scrapes the way his babe with the sweet caboose and her sisters could. "Definitely no place for a pretty face like yours, doll."

"I've been lucky," she said. "But life's short. Why not enjoy it while I still can?"

The server came back and took their order. Two steak sandwiches with garlic fries. After placing their order, Pauly said, "You know what? Go ahead and bring us the rest of that bottle."

* * *

Susan let the ice water trickle down her throat as she reviewed her notes. Dion's cause of death had been listed as blunt force trauma. That made sense. When he was found, it was obvious he had fallen forward, smashing his forehead on the exposed roots of the oak tree. Poor kid probably tripped on the roots, lost his balance, and wiped out. But this semicapitis muscle contusion was new information. She swore it hadn't been there when she'd accessed this report before. Just to be certain, she checked the medical website again.

"A blow to the back of the head might've been the coup de grace," she said aloud, confirming her suspicions, "whether it happened before or after he fell against the roots. But either way, that means it couldn't have been an accident. And besides, there was no car where he was found. So, how did he get there, and, how could that have happened?"

She ran through some scenarios in her mind. Years of watching old detective show reruns in dumpy motels after burlesque performances with her sisters had given her a healthy appreciation for the key elements of crime: motive, means, and opportunity.

"So, let's see," she said, talking it out. "Dion was well-liked, but his family wasn't. So, maybe someone wanted to harm his family. But who?"

She started with the obvious. Tapping the name Occhipinti into her browser, she came up with a long string of search results, mostly related to the winery and its offerings. She tabbed down the list. There were dozens of articles about the company's impact on the community.

STATE-OF-THE-ART COMMUNITY COLLEGE TO BE NAMED AFTER OCCHIPINTIS AFTER LAND DONATION

"At least they're doing some good with their money," Susan thought. She browsed the article, curious as to what "state-of-the-art" meant. A cutting-edge computer lab, laptops for every student, a top-quality football stadium, a spacious theater, and a culinary arts center that trained aspiring chefs and provided free lunches for both low-income students and the local food bank were among the perks of the school, built nearly a decade ago. In a community that housed wealthy agriculture families as well as migrant workers, that college seemed to be doing a lot of heavy lifting. All with the kind of PR that money couldn't buy. Though there were other small colleges in the area, none could match the prestige of Occhipinti.

Then Susan remembered one of Dom's conversations with Florence. "Something about that guy," he'd said about Dion's father. She went back to her laptop and started typing, looking for any connection between Carlo Maggioli and the Occhipintis. Soon, she had her answer.

* * *

Dom huffed as they stepped off the curb. In the crosswalk, Margaret turned. "Still there?"

He hurried across the street. "Yep," he said through thin breaths. "Right behind ya."

Stepping onto the sidewalk, he noticed several cruisers and black and white SUVs in a lot behind cyclone fencing. "Madonn', is that what I think it is? A clubhouse?"

"You mean a cop shop?" Margaret asked. "Makes sense. Library's on the other side of the block. Probably all city land. Bet there's a post office around here somewhere, too."

Dom shuddered. "I ain't fond of police stations." He slouched and turned his head out of habit. Anything to keep from attracting attention, even if he didn't have a reason to feel guilty.

"I'll protect you," Margaret chuckled. "You wanted fresh air. This place is full of it."

As they neared the building, a strawberry blonde clutching a small device raised her voice. "I need confirmation," she pleaded with a uniformed officer trying to escort her out the front door. "Chief Novak said he'd give me a quote today. What's his reaction to the news?"

"Miss Kendall," the officer said, "the chief has no comment at this time."

"Is it true that this is now a murder investigation?" she pressed, trying to step forward.

"You need to leave the premises, Miss Kendall," the officer said. "Now."

"This is public property," she countered, pointing her finger at him. "I know my rights."

"You're trespassing," he said, hovering over her. She suddenly looked miniscule.

"It's not trespassing if it's on public property," she said, standing her ground.

"It is if you've been asked to leave," he said. Four officers stood behind him. "And you have. Now go."

She snapped, "My publisher will hear about this. And our attorney. I promise you that."

The officer crossed his arms but said nothing. Defeated, the woman turned and stalked to a car parked at the sidewalk, nearly colliding with Dom and Margaret, who had to lurch out of the way. But instead of apologizing, she yanked open the door, got in, and sped away.

Dom and Margaret looked at each other, unsure of what had just happened.

"You all right?" he asked.

"Yeah. What the hell?"

"If I drove that fast outta a police station, I'd be in the clink before I made the corner."

"Right?"

They walked farther, reaching the library. A group of kids on the lawn wriggled in anticipation of story time. Dom welcomed the shade from the pine trees out front. Beneath the overhang, they found a newspaper rack.

"You got quarters?" Margaret asked, holding out her hand.

"They still make those?" He nodded to the rack as he dug in his pocket. "I got three."

"I need three more," she said.

He stuck his hand in his other pocket. "That's all I got."

She looked around. "All right," she said, holding up a quarter, "put this in when I say." She gripped the handle on the rack's door and wiggled it. Then, a nod. "Drop it in the slot."

When he did, she pushed the handle and pressed up. The door lifted and she nodded again. Dom reached in and took a paper, casually folding it under his arm as she scanned the area. Then she gently closed the door.

He smiled at her, impressed. "Where did you—"

"Don't ask," she said.

They walked to a bench in the shade and sat down. Dom unfolded the paper and spread it out on the table, like he used to do with Florence.

GARLIC HEIR DECEASED, CAUSE OF DEATH UNKNOWN read the front-page, centered over a photo of a smiling young man with curly blond hair and soft brown eyes. He was tan, fit-looking, yet still somehow childlike.

"Dion Maggioli, twenty-six has died," Margaret read. "Grandson of Ignazio Maggioli, founder of Maggioli Garlic Growers, the younger Maggioli was a company executive. It was recently announced he would take on an expanded role in the agricultural giant's daily operations."

"Good lookin' kid," Dom said, staring at the boyish smile on this young man he'd told Florence he'd find. "Such a shame."

"Interesting," Margaret noted. "They mention his grandfather, but not—"

"His father," Dom completed her thought. "I told Flo there's somethin' about that guy."

Margaret read further. "Says he went to Stanford and that he was very involved in the local community. Volunteer work. Helping the homeless. Fundraising for schools. Supporting STEM programs. Serving as a mentor to troubled high school students. Distributing meals. Liked to restore old cars. Look at this old Mustang." She tilted the newspaper toward Dom and showed him a photo of Dion in front of a slick green muscle car. "Cripes, he was young, attractive, compassionate, rich. Why would anyone want this kid dead?"

Dom scratched his head. "Seems like we keep asking ourselves that. But, everyone's the villain in someone else's story."

* * *

Draining the second bottle of Occhipinti cabernet sauvignon into Millie's glass, Pauly tilted to one side, gripping the table's edge to steady himself. Only a few drops of the wine spilled onto the tablecloth. The restaurant's lunch crowd had mostly cleared, and the newlyweds were among a handful of remaining customers. When their server came back with Pauly's credit card, he slipped it into his wallet and fished out a $20 to leave as a tip.

"You said you had a surr-prize," Millie said, raising her glass. "Remember?"

Pauly blinked, hoping his vision would come into focus. "I did," he said. "I do, Kitten."

She leaned forward, giving her husband a view of the ample bosom concealed within her mint green wraparound blouse. "So," she teased, aware she had his rapt attention, "what is it?"

Pauly did his best to pull both eyes up to her face at the same time, nearly succeeding.

"Kitten," he said, "I …" He glanced outside and saw a sign on the store across the street.

FINE JEWELRY

Pawn Shop

Appraisals

"I'm gonna buy you somethin' nice," he said.

"Ooh, somethin' nice?" she echoed.

"Just because," Pauly said, gripping her hand and clumsily bringing it to his lips. He planted a sloppy kiss on it, then squeezed it again. He held it firm, steadying his wobble. "Whenever you're ready to go."

She took a final sip of her wine. "Well, I think I'm ready to go now," she announced, reaching for her purse. "You good?"

Pauly stood, still woozy. "I think I need to use the can again," he said. "Be right back." He teetered toward the restroom, the hall narrowing and widening as he walked. He opened the door and was greeted by the iron bars of the old jail cell. The image sobered him, and he drew a long breath before proceeding to do his business. When he was done, he washed his hands and splashed cold water on his face. Still a little tired from this morning, he saw his reflection in the mirror. Gray streaks in his dark curls and creases on his forehead. But overall, he saw a man who was happy. The door opened and another man entered. Pauly wiped his face with a towel and went back to Millie. He laced his fingers in hers and escorted her out the door.

"So, where are we going?" she asked as they waited at the curb for the light to turn green. When it did, Pauly led her into the crosswalk.

"Over there," he said. "Let's find you a nice piece of jewelry."

"Really?" Millie squealed as she clutched his arm. "Oh, Pauly, how sweet!"

"Look, I know this ain't no honeymoon," he said, patting her hand. "But that doesn't mean we can't find a nice little memento to mark the occasion."

As they stepped onto the sidewalk, they heard loud voices coming from the direction of the store. Three large men stood at the doorway, the one in front wagging a finger at someone inside. And Pauly recognized him from the airport and the parking lot at the gala.

"You got until tomorrow at noon," the man yelled. "Have it ready!"

One of the men in the back leaned forward, pushing himself into the doorway. Then he held up a backpack and pointed to it. "To-mor-row," he said slowly. Then he put up two fingers and made a slashing motion across his neck. "Or you get a new necktie."

Pauly froze. Not only did he recognize the man, he was quite familiar with that phrase and didn't want to be made while he was with Millie. The three turned around, stumbling over each other. As they righted themselves, Pauly pushed Millie against the building, painted with a mural of the old train depot that once stood there. He cradled the back of her head against the image of a locomotive, careful to conceal her face, and worked his tongue over hers until he heard the men pass. Shortly, doors opened and closed. The squeal of tires let him know they were gone.

"What was that about," Millie asked, straightening her hair.

Pauly watched the truck speed off, weaving and passing oncoming traffic. "You know what a necktie is? A cravat?"

"That thing that goes around your neck when you wear a suit?"

Pauly shook his head. "No, baby," he looked over his shoulder, "a necktie is when you slit a guy's throat and then you reach up and pull his tongue down, so it hangs outta his neck."

"Gross," Millie gasped. "Did you ever—"

"Some things, you shouldn't ask."

She nodded. "All right, but why would anyone—"

"It's what you get when you squeal. *Jittari i vermiceddi,* as they say in Sicily."

"Ji-what now?"

"It means vomit the pasta, spill your guts," Pauly said.

"Colorful," Millie said, holding her stomach.

"Look, doll, I dunno if we should go into this here hock shop," Pauly said. "I got a bad feelin' about it. I don't wanna get mixed up in that business again."

His stomach clenched, knowing he was lying to his new bride.

"It's all right," Millie agreed. "I understand."

"But I promise, I'll buy you somethin' real special before we dust outta this town."

She smiled. "I'll hold you to that," she said.

He pulled her close and kissed her. "You can hold me to anything, Mrs. Molinaro."

They smooched like teenagers. "Come on," she finally said, "let's get back to the house."

They started past the pawn shop, but Pauly turned. "This way," he said, leading her down the sidewalk. They walked the few blocks to the old blue Victorian and climbed the steps. He opened the door and led her inside. Dom, Margaret, and Susan were in the parlor, stretched on the couches, the television in the background. Susan's laptop, a pitcher of lemonade, glasses, and a *Town Crier* sat on the coffee table.

Pauly raised his brows, hoping to speak to Dom privately. But before he could get Dom's attention, Margaret asked, "How was lunch?"

"Ooh, we went to that city hall restaurant," Millie gushed as Pauly closed the door and locked it, glancing through the glass and making a quick check of the sidewalk, just in case. "And get this. It used to be a jail and there are *cells* in the restrooms. Isn't that wild?"

Dom looked at Pauly, who mouthed, "Don't ask."

"Sounds fun," Susan said. "Hey, you'll never guess what I found out. I was just about to tell Dom and Margaret, so I'm glad you're here."

Pauly poured Millie some lemonade and then took a seat beside her on the other couch.

"So," Susan continued, "it seems Dion took a hit to the back of his skull."

"I thought he fell forward," Millie said.

"He did," Susan clarified. "But now the report shows a blow to the back of his head, too."

"Is that what killed him?" Dom asked.

"It's doesn't say," Susan said.

"But you can't rule it out," Pauly chimed in. "Happens all the time. If you know what you're doin', you can whack a guy in the back of the head, hit just the right spot, no blood."

Dom picked up, "And let's say the guy happens to fall forward, on something solid."

"Like tree roots," Margaret said.

"Exactly," said Susan.

"You think that's what happened?" Millie asked.

"Hard to say," Susan said. "The autopsy doesn't specify. But he had injuries consistent with both a blow to the back of the head and a forward fall. But," she said, "that's not all."

Millie raised a brow. "Oh?"

"First of all, he had a note in his pocket that read BM/C."

"Da fuck does that mean?" Dom asked. "Oh, ladies, pardon my French."

Susan laughed. "Honey, we've heard worse. And I have no idea what it means. But remember how Florence said there was something about Carlo she didn't trust?"

Dom sipped his lemonade. "Yeah?"

"Well, I looked him up," Susan said. "Not only is he not part of the company, but they don't even own most of the land they're using to grow their garlic."

"So, who does?" Margaret asked.

"The Occhipintis," Susan said.

"How is that?" Pauly asked.

"Looks like they made a very large loan to Carlo, about twenty-five years ago," Susan said. "In exchange, they hold the deed to the land and the Maggiolis pay rent to use it."

"Susie, you are one sharp cookie," Dom said. "Way to crack the dots."

The other four turned and looked at Dom, confused by his metaphor mixing.

"Dom," Pauly said, seizing the opportunity, "I wanna talk—"

AND NOW, WE HAVE BREAKING NEWS.

Everyone turned toward the TV. Dom found the remote and increased the volume. A man with shoulder-length hair was shown on a tarmac, then cuffed and stuffed into the back of a police cruiser. Pauly stepped closer to read the scrawl.

CARLO MAGGIOLI ARRESTED FOR SON'S MURDER.

| 15 |

Gloria Maggioli slugged back the rest of her gin and tonic, then clumsily set the crystal glass on the end table. The tumbler wobbled as she stared at the television, numb to what was being said. At least the authorities had been kind enough to alert her that they'd be taking Carlo into custody when he got off his international flight. She watched as he tossed his stringy hair over his shoulder and scrunched into the back of the squad car, hands cuffed behind him.

"I told you," Gloria slurred, a manicured finger wagging at the television, "your secrets would catch up to you and destroy you some day."

She tottered to her feet, clutching her cane to steady herself. A collection of photographs adorned the mantel. Gloria and Carlo ready to slice into their wedding cake. Gloria, Carlo, and Dion posing for a family portrait. Dion with Ignazio, atop a tractor and rumbling through the garlic fields. The extended Maggioli family, minus Carlo, at the ribbon cutting for their new office. Dion's graduation from Stanford, resplendent in his cap and gown. Gloria closed her eyes tight, wishing it would bring him back. But she knew it was futile.

"Carlo Maggioli, who had been removed from the Maggioli Garlic Growers board years ago, did not resist arrest for the murder of his son …" the television droned.

Gloria opened her eyes and stared at the wedding photo. Her friends from the neighborhood had tried to talk her out of marrying Carlo. For more than two decades, she'd wished she'd listened. But she was naïve and carefree. Carlo was wealthy beyond imagination. A risk-taker who didn't care for convention. Not to mention charismatic and sexy. He made her feel like the only woman in the world. Until that dreadful morning when she learned it was a lie.

"I'll tell her to get rid of it," he'd pleaded.

"No," Gloria cried from the doorway. "Do not hurt that baby. That innocent soul has nothing to do with this."

"I'll make her give it up," Carlo promised.

"No," she said, her voice trembling, but determined not to wake Dion. "It's your responsibility. You will care for it."

"But it will disgrace my family," Carlo argued.

She grabbed her riding helmet and spun. "Your family? What about me? Your wife?"

"Gloria," he begged, "don't leave like this. I never meant to hurt you."

She flung the door open and stomped toward the stables. "Maybe you should've thought about that before you went off to fuck the Rosettos' maid."

With a desperate wail, Gloria swung her cane into the wedding photo. The glass within the frame shattered, sending shards in every direction. Next, she struck the ceramic candlesticks on the mantel, a wedding gift from Ignazio and Adalgisa. She smashed them into tiny fragments, until only dust remained. The final victim of her seething rage was the nineteenth-century Empire clock with brass chimes, a gift for their twenty-fifth anniversary. "Yours until the end of time," Carlo had it inscribed. Gloria lifted her cane, then hesitated. Instead, she grabbed the clock and chucked it onto the polished oak floor, splitting it into quadrants. The chimes resounded eerily, echoing on the wooden floor as she swayed from the gin's grasp. She stood over the detritus she'd created. Groomed to be an apologetic soother, her default emotion was shame. But she was oddly proud of what she'd done. Something within her finally felt relief.

"Ma'am," called a voice behind her. "Is everything all right?"

Her heaving chest eased, a sense of calm overtaking her. "Ingrid," she said, turning to face her housekeeper with a smile, "please see that this gets this cleaned up. And I'd like Timothy to drive me to Sainte Cecelia's."

* * *

Dom looked out the window as the others buzzed about Carlo's arrest. A sleek Mercedes slowed to a stop across the street. "I'll be right back," he said, heading to the front door.

"Where you goin'?" Pauly called after him. "We need to talk about—"

But Dom was already shuffling down the steps. He mustered a jog to cross the street as the driver's door swung open. "Mrs. Rosetto," he said, offering her his hand. "I mean, Giuseppina."

"Oh," she said, startled as she swung her gams around and set two silk pumps the shade of spring roses on the concrete. "Dom, what a pleasant surprise. Do you live around here?"

"Oh, just visiting," he explained as he helped her from the car. She was elegant in a deep mauve A-line dress, fitted at the waist, with a large pearl necklace, earrings, and pin in her pillbox hat. "Renting," he began, "nearby." A car approached and he guided her to the curb.

"Well, how lovely," she said, popping the trunk with her remote. "I'm dropping off items for the compassion center. It's just around the corner but there's no parking today." As the lid of her trunk lifted, he spied cases of canned fruits and vegetables, boxes of pasta, and jars of peanut butter, jam, and spaghetti sauce.

"Oh, let me to help you," he offered, hoisting a load of canned goods.

She deliberately unfolded a rolling cart she'd grabbed from the trunk. "How kind of you."

Dom felt a tightness in his spine as he loaded the goods into the basket of the cart, but he maintained a happy face. *"Non c'e problema,"* he said as his lower back began to twitch.

"Grazie," she replied with a smile as she closed the trunk.

"Besides, I saw you and wanted to say hello since we got interrupted at the gala the other day," Dom said, now lugging the cart along the sidewalk.

"Speaking of that," she began, "I wanted to ask you. And please don't think I'm butting in where I don't belong. But I saw you talking to a young man in the parking lot."

Dom winced, partly from his lumbar region seizing up and partly because he feared what might be coming next. "Oh?"

She checked over her shoulder. "Listen," she whispered, "it's none of my business. But you don't want to get mixed up with someone like Onorato D'Agostini. That boy is trouble."

"Oh, is that his name?" Dom wondered aloud. "I don't really know him. We thought he was one of those Valentinos," he said.

She stopped and looked at him, perplexed. "Valentinos?"

"Yeah, you know, the guys who park your car?"

A soft laugh fluttered from her mouth. "Oh, a valet," she said, amused. "How charming."

"Right. A *val-et,*" Dom said, accentuating the word. "That's definitely what I meant."

"Well," she said as they walked toward Central Road, "he's mixed up in things you don't want to be involved in."

"Like what?" Dom blurted before he could stop himself. "If you don't mind me asking."

"Things good people don't do. Unforgiveable things that cost men their souls."

"Business," Dom said knowingly.

She nodded. "And it's a shame. He never knew his father, but his mother was a darling."

"How do you know her?"

"She worked for my husband, Antonio, and I," she explained as they waited for the light.

"Dio riposi la sua anima," Dom said.

"God rest his soul, indeed," she replied. They began to cross. "Antonio was a good man. Hired Onorato's mother, Belinda, just before she found out she was pregnant. Poor thing had nowhere to go. Abandoned by her family because of her *situation*. I never wanted domestics.

But I knew it would help her and it also gave me more time to work in the community. Belinda had a hard pregnancy, and a hard delivery. That boy was more than ten pounds at birth."

"Yeesh," Dom said, pulling the cart up the curb.

"Belinda did her best to raise him," Giuseppina recalled. "But he fell in with the wrong element, if you know what I mean."

"I do," Dom said, his arm numb from lugging the cart.

"Anyway, she died a few years ago," she said, "and I'm afraid Onorato never recovered. In fact, I think it drove him further into that life."

They slowed to a stop as a line had formed outside the door to the compassion center. Giuseppina motioned to Dom to follow her around the building.

"I like to be anonymous," she explained. "Come on. We'll use the service entrance."

Dom huffed to keep up with her, the cart wobbling as he loped along. "You were saying, about this D'Agostini kid, he don't have a father?"

"Oh, he *has* one," she said as they turned into the alley. "He's just never been acknowledged. That family would never allow it."

Dom's dark brows raised. "Sorry, I don't follow."

She leaned closer and Dom smelled the delicate fragrance of white roses and bergamot on her neck. "See," she explained, "Antonio told me on his deathbed that Onorato's father is—"

Dom raised his brows again, but she suddenly withdrew.

"Maybe I shouldn't say," Giuseppina whispered. "But he's very well known in this town. Used to do business with my husband. And Antonio was *well-compensated* to keep it quiet."

Dom's head began to spin. *A secret love child? But whose?* She frowned. "Oh," Dom said, "your secret's safe with me. I'll be honest with you, Giuseppina. I'm here to find out what happened to someone my ex-wife knew."

Her perfectly lined lips turned upward into a smile. "Ex-wife? How charitable of you."

"It's her nephew," Dom explained. "Well, not really her nephew. The son of an old friend. Anyway, something happened to him, and I told her I'd find out."

"Anything I can do to help?"

"That's generous of you," he said. "I don't think I could ask."

She pulled a calling card from her purse. "My pleasure," she said, setting it in his hand. "I know a lot about this town. More than people realize. You need anything at all, just let me know. Besides, how else can I repay you for your kindness in helping me lug these goods down here?"

The service door opened. In flawless Spanish, Giuseppina spoke to the woman in the doorway. Two men took the cart and Giuseppina stepped into the doorway to chat with the woman. Dom wasn't sure what to do with himself. He wondered about Onorato's paternity, and why Giuseppina had clammed up. He ran his thumb over the calling card she'd given him. Mrs. Giuseppina Rosetto, it read in neat, gold script and embossed with a golden rose. He tucked it into his wallet as the men returned the cart.

"Adios, Marisol," Giuseppina said with a wave. "I'll pick up the cart next time."

Dom smiled as she approached him.

"I'm sorry to keep you waiting," she said.

"Nah, I don't mind. Lemme walk you to your car."

"Oh, I've got a meeting at the chamber," she said, "up the block."

"Well," Dom said, "then I guess this is goodbye."

She extended her hand, which he shook gently. "For now," she said. He held her hand a bit longer, then let it go. "Thanks again. And please. Do not hesitate to call if I can help—"

Her cell phone rang in her purse, prompting her to roll her eyes. "Oh, I'm so sorry."

"I won't keep you," Dom said as she fumbled for her phone. "Enjoy the rest of your day." He waved and then walked back down the block, surprised that he was humming to himself.

Giuseppina stood on the sidewalk, her phone pressed to one ear and her hand to the other. "Darling, I'm sorry, it's hard to hear. Did you say *Carlo?*"

* * *

Pauly was waiting on the porch as Dom gingerly climbed the steps. "Where'd you go?"

Dom rubbed his back. "See that Mercedes across the street?"

Pauly peered over Dom's shoulder. "Yeah, so?"

"That's Giuseppina's. You know, the Apple Fritter Lady?"

"And?"

"And," Dom said as he collapsed into a chair, "I saw her pull up and thought I'd say hello. We didn't really get to talk at the gala with everything going on. And it's a good thing I did." He dug into his pocket and pulled out her calling card.

"Dominic, you sly dog, you got her digits?" Pauly said, smacking Dom's arm.

"What? No. I mean, yeah, I did, but it's not like that. At least, I don't *think* it is."

Pauly's face squished into a confused stare. "You lost me."

Dom waved the calling card. "I recognized her car from the bakery. I saw her pull up across the street and went out to say hello. She had a bunch of food to donate to the shelter, so I helped her carry it. And when I did, we started talking. I told her I was here looking for someone. Then she said she has a lot of connections here, and to call if I need help."

Pauly sized him up. "Well, that was nice."

"Right? And, she said that Onorato is bad news."

"No shit," Pauly said, shrugging it off with a laugh. "That's what I've been trying to tell you. I saw him today while I was out with Millie. And I realized I saw him at the airport when we first got here, too."

"Huh. I don't take that kid for a pilot."

"Not like that. Both places, he was puttin' the squeeze on somebody. Doin' a shakedown."

"No shit? You think that's the job he wants us to do?"

"Makes sense. C'mon, we been around. We saw through that guy from the jump. Like lookin' at younger versions of us."

"But that ain't all," Dom said. "Here's where it gets interesting. She said he has questionable paternity."

"Mi scusi?"

"Get this. His father is from an important family around here, but he was never acknowledged," Dom explained. "Born out of wedlock and raised by a single mother, who just so happened to be Giuseppina's housekeeper."

Pauly's eyes widened. "Wow. Did she say who his father is?"

"No, and I think she was just about to, but something spooked her, and she got quiet."

"I see," Pauly said, watching the traffic. "So, who do you think it is?"

"I figure we got two possibilities, at least as far as the families go, right?"

"Yeah, seems like it."

"So, let's think about these families and how an illegitimate son might cause problems," Dom said. "Does it hurt one more than the other?"

Pauly leaned forward. "Or is there something in their history that might seem weird or mysterious. Hard to explain?"

A city bus lumbered by. On its side was a large ad for Occhipinti Vineyards, a smaller version of the billboard near the da Conceicaos' estate. Pauly rolled his eyes toward Dom.

"You think…"

Dom shook his head. "I dunno," he said. "My gut says no. Remember what Big Mike said. The Occhipintis don't get involved in anything unless it's going to benefit them somehow."

"Right," Pauly said, "but maybe someone didn't think that through. You know, in the heat of passion, sometimes people forget their priorities."

"True, but you saw how they were at that gala. That family is focused. And I don't think they're the kind to lose sight of their priorities. Now," Dom said, "think about what Big Mike said about Carlo," Dom said, looking at Pauly.

"He's not known for making the best decisions," they said in unison.

"And Dion's father has been conspicuously out of the family business," Pauly noted.

"For the last twenty-five or so years," Dom concluded. "Right about the time—"

* * *

Gloria Maggioli dragged her cane across the narthex of Sainte Cecelia's, generating a lopsided cadence that echoed from its thick walls. Her gin worn off, she was more stable now, focused on a pew in the northern transept. This was her spot. She sat here with Dion from his baptism and first communion to his catechism and confirmation. Carlo would come along in the beginning, but over time, he'd chosen other things over his faith. Eventually, Carlo became a C&E Catholic, only attending service on Christmas and Easter, and the occasional wedding or funeral. Gloria wondered if the shame of fathering another woman's child had made it too painful for Carlo to be in this cathedral where they'd exchanged their vows.

She crossed the nave, genuflected at the altar, steadied herself, and headed to the transept. Stained-glass murals refracted multicolored light, guiding her like a kaleidoscope splattering of holiness cast upon the stone floor. At her pew, she bowed again, then sat. She reached into her purse for her rosary, arranged in decades of aquamarine and sterling silver. The centerpiece was a representation of St. Catherine of Siena set against a large, emerald-cut aquamarine stone.

It was a fitting choice in many ways. St. Catherine had been paralyzed from the waist down after suffering a stroke in her final days. "Build a cell inside your mind from which you can never flee," she famously advised her fellow Dominican, Raymond of Capua, when asked what one should do when confronted with trouble. A patron saint of illness, sexual temptation, miscarriages, and those ridiculed for their piety, St. Catherine was a martyr without martyrdom. Much like Gloria, long-suffering in silence due to Carlo's sins and fiercely dedicated to her obligations. But in her most urgent obligation, looking after Dion, she had failed. At twenty-six, he was a grown man. But a mother who buries a child is scarred forever, frozen in time by her grief, paralyzed by the unanswerable question, "What more could I have done?"

Gloria looped the rosary through her fingers and clasped her hands together, bringing them to rest below her chin. The space was looming yet intimate, filled with reverent calm. She closed her eyes, centering herself. The tightness in her chest and shoulders eased into the tranquility as she made the sign of the cross and expelled a breath. Slipping the crucifix between her fingers, she began the Apostle's Creed.

"I believe in God, the Father Almighty, Creator of Heaven and Earth…"

"… and in Jesus Christ, His only son, our Lord …" came a lilting voice to her right. Gloria opened her eyes and saw Rialta Occhipinti on the pew beside her, clutching her own rosary. After exchanging a brief but friendly smile, they continued their prayers in unison.

* * *

Pauly jumped when his phone rang. "Dom," he said from the couch where they'd nodded off, their bellies stuffed with enchiladas and *queso fundido* from the restaurant around the corner with the faded serapes and paper lanterns on the patio. "It's him."

Dom shook himself awake and checked his watch. Nearly nine o'clock. The girls had gone to touch up their roots and do each other's nails. The phone rang again. "Answer it," he said. "Find out what he wants."

Pauly did as he was told. "Uh-huh," he said, reaching for a notepad on the end table. "Sure. We can do that. Day after tomorrow? Okay, what time?"

Dom felt his pulse tighten, the way it always did before a job in the old days. They'd done a million of them. But no matter how many they did, it always felt like the first time.

"I got it," Pauly said, jotting something down. "We'll see you then. No, no, thank you."

Dom spread his hands. "Well?"

"We got a job," Pauly said. "Thirty large apiece, and then some."

Dom stewed.

"What?" Pauly asked. "You got a problem with it? One last job."

"The last job was supposed to be the last job."

Pauly shrugged. "I know. But you told Flo—"

"Dammit," Dom said, twitching. "I know."

Pauly laid a hand on Dom's arm. "It'll be worth it. Thirty large, and I got a feeling this is gonna be our ticket to finding out what happened to Dion."

Dom stared into the distance. "I hope you're right."

| 16 |

Kate Kendall gave it two more rings, then hung up. "Someone's going to answer," she snapped as she dialed the police station again. Greeted by a busy signal, she ended the call with a frustrated groan. The newsroom—if you could call it that—was quiet, her editor and publisher off for their weekly lunch meeting. They rented this workspace to have a bona fide office on the town's main avenue, but most of her work was done on the beat or in her apartment. The office was just a place to receive mail or meet with her publisher, editor, and tiny staff.

She had worked her way up, freelancing and stringing at first. Covering community events like ribbon cuttings and profiling seniors who offered their wisdom about the town's good old days. Later, she convinced her editor to let her tackle tougher subjects like the need for more resources to address the growing homeless population, a high-speed rail plan, and efforts to modernize the agriculture industry. It meant a lot of glad-handing, city council networking, and poring over tedious committee meeting minutes. But she was eager to make her mark on this small community she'd adopted after college. Her big city journalism degree gave her a false sense of cockiness. It took one press conference with Ignazio Maggioli to set her straight.

"Why isn't Carlo on your board anymore?" she'd asked with smirky confidence from the front row after listening to a prepared speech about record sales figures and new products.

A stony scowl, a subtle wave of his wrinkled hand, and a non-optional invitation to relocate to the back of the room, accompanied by two burly, silent men, followed. A rookie mistake, but she got the message. Pick your battles, use alternative research methods if you think a source won't give you what you need, and always save the "gotcha" question for last.

She paged down her screen to review her notes. The Maggiolis sure had their names attached to a lot of news, business, and property in this town. But through research, she'd discovered that Carlo had taken out a series of loans about twenty-five years ago. And there had been small monthly payments to a corporation, listed as FSI, since then. Carlo had made the first few payments from his Maggioli Garden Growers business account. But soon, he was removed from MGG, not appearing to serve in any capacity. And Ignazio had taken over the payments. Kate thought it was odd that Dion, in charge of MGG's daily operations, wasn't the signatory.

She also noted that around the time he took out the loans, he set up a trust for a woman named Belinda Smith. Carlo often made donations to people in need and charities, so it wasn't unusual. But it wasn't common, either. Kate hoped to contact her, but there were hundreds of Smiths, and besides, she didn't seem to reside in this town or any town that surrounded it. No property owned or rented by someone with that name. When she finally tracked her down, it was through a death notice. Belinda Smith had succumbed to breast cancer. And the trail went cold.

Kate's next effort was to identify the corporation that held the loans, FSI. But that was a tangled mess of shell companies and DBAs. As far as she could tell, they were headquartered in the area, but there was no physical address. Just a post office box in the next town over, not far from the country club. But she'd been to the post office several times. And it appeared that the box was stuffed full of envelopes whenever she'd visited. Another dead end.

Finally, she kept trying to dig up any information that would indicate Carlo had a criminal record. He was clearly hiding something. Why else would he have been removed from the family business without a word? And with a newborn at home? There were a few moving violations, and he'd dutifully paid the fines. One disorderly misconduct incident in a local sports bar which had been dismissed. A small claims suit against a building contractor, later settled out of court. But that appeared to be it. Either the reclusive but suspiciously shifty Carlo Maggioli was a law-abiding citizen, or he benefitted from the best lawyers—and possibly judges—the Maggiolis could buy. But Kate had developed a profound trust in her instincts in journalism school. And her gut told her it was the latter. Guys like that always seemed to get away with everything. And Carlo was no doubt on the wrong side of something. But what?

"Hey," said a voice over her shoulder. "You've got some mail."

Kate turned to see Zack, her publisher's nephew, holding a stack of envelopes. Still in high school, he did chores around the office. He had dreams of a front-page byline someday, but, due to his penchant for conspiracy theories, Kate politely dismissed him when he went on a tangent about winning the Pulitzer for investigative reporting.

"Oh," she said, startled. "Thanks."

"That's the one you've been waiting for, right?" his adolescent voice squeaked.

She looked at the envelope.

Office of Information Policy

U.S. Department of Justice

Washington D.C.

Kate snatched the envelope. "Yes," she said, awed. "Thank you."

"Yeah, I thought it looked kind of official, being from Washing—"

But Kate didn't hear him. She was fumbling through her desk drawer, pushing aside rogue sweetener packets, plastic-wrapped foam cups of ramen, and a stash of hair ties she never remembered to use. Finally, she dug deep enough to retrieve her letter opener. She wielded it carefully, aligning the flap with the blade. Then she stopped, slowly raising her eyes to him.

"Do you mind?" she asked.

"Oh," he said softly and pointing behind him with his thumb. "I'll just..."

She glared until he looked away.

"I need to clean out the coffee pot," he announced then walked off.

Kate took a deep breath, eager with anticipation as she slid the blade under the envelope flap. With a single, satisfying slice, she slit it neatly. Her hands shook as she removed the page inside and scanned the text.

Dear Ms. Kendall, in response to your request, yadda yadda…

She went over the typewritten lines multiple times, the words she was reading failing to register. Finally, she saw it.

FSI, aka Figlio Segreto, Inc., owned by L. S. Occhipinti.

Lazaro Occhipinti? Why would he be taking payments from the Maggiolis? And for twenty-five years?

She swigged the cold coffee in her mug and set it on the desk.

"Figlio Segreto," Kate recited under her breath. *"Segreto,* that means segregated… separate? No, secluded?"

She stared at the page, words swirling as she tried to work it out. *"Segreto,"* she mused.

Then she saw it. Right there in black and white.

"Figlio," she gasped. "That means son."

She re-read it to be sure. It all made sense now. She just had to fill in the details.

"Figlio Segreto," she said, louder now. "Secret son."

* * *

Jacob Novak looked up from his paperwork when his secretary knocked at his door.

"Chief," she said, "you have several calls to return to Kate Kend—"

"I know, Darcy," he said. "She's been quite persistent today."

"Is there anything that you'd like me to tell her the next time she—"

"No, thank you," he said, waving his hand and returning to his paperwork.

"All right, well, I'll just—"

"Thank you," he said curtly, prompting her to back out and close the door. He resumed reviewing Carlo Maggioli's file. Maybe this would be the case that got him promoted out of this small town with a big sense of self. Policing a town with little violent crime wasn't much of a challenge. But it paid well, and he enjoyed being somewhat of a celebrity everywhere he went. The country club, rotary meetings, and, of course, the Occhipintis' annual harvest gala. He got to serve as a judge in community cook-offs, present checks to charitable organizations, and be hailed as a hero when he visited school assemblies. Come on, who doesn't like cops?

He also knew how to maintain a certain level of loyalty, and when to look the other way. Even when it meant compromising his integrity in this small town of powerful businessmen. Once he'd done it, he found himself constantly balancing the oath he took with his own interests. It was hard to reconcile, and more than anything, he wanted that inner conflict to disappear. Hopefully this case would be the key. He was adjusting his reading glasses when his cell rang.

"Laz," he said, "how are you?"

"Well, it's not the worst day of my life," his old friend and sometime golf partner said.

Novak chuckled. "I guess not. What can I do for you? Or have I done enough?"

"Jake," said Lazaro, "I'm wondering how things are going with the case against Carlo."

"Looks solid. He has a motive. Being cut out of the family business in favor of his son."

"I heard—don't ask how—that he may hold deeds that revert to his heir upon his death."

Novak sat up straight. "Is that right?"

"You might want to look into that," Lazaro added. "And with his heir now deceased…"

"Interesting," Novak said, jotting on a notepad. "And let's just say, he's made some questionable choices over the years."

"Oh, I'm not sure I know what you mean, Jake," Lazaro said, then laughed. "But I'm certain you'll see that he's held accountable."

Novak was silent for a moment, running through his own questionable choices. He could easily haul in Lazaro's own sons—and Lazaro, too, truth be told—for a litany of offenses. But his choice had been made. And, like the rest of this town, the Occhipintis owned him, too.

"I'll do that," Novak finally said, swallowing hard.

"I knew I could count on you, Jake," Lazaro said.

"You bet," Novak said, filled with self-loathing. "Give my best to Rialta and the kids."

"I will," Lazaro said. "Chavonne is downtown today. Lunch at the rotary club, I believe."

* * *

Chavonne picked at her plate. The Caesar salad here was always disappointing. She heard her phone buzz within her purse, but ignored it, knowing exactly who it was.

"So, no one knows who bought the land?" asked a gray-haired man whose name Chavonne hadn't bothered to learn. She sized him up as he sat across from her. It was always the same group of busy-body citizens on brigade at these luncheons. She and Dion were often the only ones in their age group. Mostly bored housewives who needed a project to feel useful and business owners who cared more about lining their pockets than serving the collective needs of their community.

"No," replied Mayor Denise Watson. "Not yet. I expect we won't know for a while."

"And did you hear about Carlo?" asked another lady in a short-sleeved coral jacket and pleated white pants straight out of a Sag Harbor catalog.

Mayor Watson cleared her throat softly and turned her eyes to Chavonne.

Aware of her tablemates' attention, Chavonne frowned and sighed. "It's all so sad," she said, sniffing into a tissue. "Dion was such a good man, with a very bright future ahead."

Chair legs scraped the floor behind her and soon she felt a pair of comforting hands on her shoulders. "Don't … cry … *mia nipote*," Ubaldo said in his halting speech, patting her gently. "What's done … is … done."

Albert Watson dug into his pocket and produced a handkerchief. When he offered it to Chavonne, she recalled the day she'd met Dion at Starbucks, and her tears intensified.

"Thank you," she managed through sniffles. "I'm sorry. It's just such a shock."

"I can't believe his own father—" started the woman in the coral jacket.

"We don't know that for sure," Mayor Watson cautioned.

"Well," the gray-haired man across from Chavonne said, "I think I speak for many of us when I say I wouldn't be surprised."

Chavonne clutched her uncle's hand on her shoulder. All her life, she'd heard that Ubaldo had a "compromised mental capacity," or whatever people said when they were trying to be polite. Others avoided him because his differences made them uncomfortable. But she'd only known him to be generous and compassionate, with gentlemanly manners and an ability to smile with gratitude no matter what was happening. While others, even Nunzio and Silvestro, scoffed and whispered, he treated her like a princess. Dion had only met her uncle a handful of times but was one of the few people to show him respect. Asking about his shoes or what he'd had for lunch, listening raptly, and engaging in conversation. Patiently waiting while her uncle found the words he wanted to say. They'd tried to keep their relationship quiet, but didn't care that Ubaldo knew. *Who would he tell?*

"Well," Chavonne said, lifting her wine glass, "I hope the police solve the case soon."

Murmurs circulated around the table as everyone enjoyed their Occhipinti Vineyards pinot grigio. Nearby, Giuseppina Rosetto honed an eye on Chavonne, then sipped her wine.

* * *

"So let me get this straight," Dom said. "We're hitting the whole block?"

Pauly eased back in the dining chair in the sunny Victorian and fiddled with his coffee cup. "Yes. Well, not just us. We're just doing one side of the street. Two hits. One apiece."

"Wait a minute," Dom said, leaning forward. "We're doing these alone?"

"Yeah, so we can get it done faster. We're gonna be on a tight schedule."

"I dunno, Pauly. We ain't exactly young guys, you know?"

"You sayin' you can't do it by yourself?"

Dom ran his hand through his hair. "No, I ... it's been a long time, that's all."

"Not that long," Pauly reminded him.

"You're right," Dom said, "but that still don't mean we're young."

"You're as old as you feel, says my lovely wife," Pauly said with a smile.

"Yeah, I've heard how young you feel," Dom quipped. "Thanks."

"Look, I think we can do it," Pauly said. "How hard could it be? The shops are practically right next to each other. You go into the first shop, make the hit, collect the dough. At the same time, I'm at the second shop, doing the same thing. We meet at the car, then head to the drop."

"And where is that?"

"Some restaurant. Mili-something," Pauly said.

"Millie, like your wife? That's weird."

"I never thought about it," Pauly said, "but no, it's some old restaurant up the block."

"Wait, wait," Dom said, "the drop is up the block?"

"This town ain't that big, Dom," Pauly explained.

"And while we do this, where are the other guys?"

"Across the street a little farther, doin' the same thing."

"Really thought my loan sharking days were behind me," Dom said.

"One more job," Pauly replied.

Dom picked up his cup. "That's what we said last time. Look where it got us."

Pauly rubbed his fingers over his wedding ring. "I ain't complainin'. That last job brought me the best payoff of my life. And it's thirty large. Each. You'll be set."

Dom sipped his coffee, still torn.

"We can find out who killed Dion," Pauly reasoned. "Ain't that why we're here?"

Dom emptied the cup. As the coffee settled in his stomach, it was the acidity of his words that stung the most. "You're right. Let's do it."

Pauly clamped a hand over Dom's arm and gave it a hearty tap. Then he dialed his phone. "We're in."

Dom listened to Pauly go over the plan with Onorato. Collecting loans owed to Carlo to prevent him from paying back his loan to the Occhipintis was shady. But what really bothered him was the fact that Carlo had been arrested for his own son's murder. Illegitimate business deals were one thing. But bumping off your own son was elite territory in their lifestyle. Reserved for the worst of the worst. He couldn't help thinking of Florence, how a friend of hers could get mixed up with a guy like that. Then he remembered that he and Pauly were guys like that. Dom wondered what Florence might think about what he'd just committed to do. He went back to his room, sat on the bed, and pulled out the calling card. With shaky fingers, he dialed.

"Giuseppina," he said when she picked up, "it's Dom. I wanna take you up on that offer."

| 17 |

Eufrasio watched a pair of Swainson's hawks soar over the field down the hill from his estate. Pursuing mice, he supposed, as he watched one swoop down and snare a plump rodent within its sharp talons. He'd come to appreciate the cycle of life displayed daily in the area he called home. Sometimes it was as simple as hunt or be hunted. Grow and evolve or stagnate in the old ways and die, as many businesses—large and small—had done over the years. He'd seen enough in this community to know that time might bring heavy rains, but that rain also nurtures the crops. Adaptation is necessary to survival, for those who dared to make the effort.

He sipped his morning espresso and turned up the collar of his robe. The fog had thickened over the hills and the moist, garlic-scented air chilled his nose and hands. He went through his grocery list in his mind, still sharp even in his 70s, noting what he'd need for tonight's meal. Beneath the shade of his leafy madrone, he watched the hawk, now perched on a post, tear into its breakfast.

* * *

Dom fought back a surge of heartburn as he leaned to tie his shoes. When he was done, he sat up and caught his breath. "You schmoes ready?" he asked over the din of breakfast dishes.

"What did Giuseppina say?" Pauly asked as he pulled on his sweatshirt.

"To meet her at this address," Dom said, handing Pauly a slip of paper.

"What kinda place is it?" Pauly squinted at it. "A house? A business?"

"Neither," Dom said. "A set of three abandoned buildings. I guess they were going to be part of a house, but the owner defaulted, and the property went into foreclosure. Then someone else bought it, but they also foreclosed. So, they've been sitting empty for a long time."

"Why does she want to meet there?"

"Not sure," Dom explained. "Something in Dion's autopsy. She said she had a hunch."

They filed into the rental car and Dom drove to the property on Bel Monte. The gray cement buildings were easy to spot, set back from the road, rising from mounds of tall, yellowing grass. Blue tarps draped randomly over the roofs, rippling in the morning breeze. As Dom pulled onto Collina Avenue, he spotted Giuseppina's Mercedes. She wore slim, dark jeans, a black twin set festooned with an amethyst brooch, and a neat black cloche, fastened with an amethyst pin along the lace band. Her silver hair rippled in bouncy waves on her shoulders.

"Madonn'," Dom said aloud, entranced by her elegance and panache.

"Good morning," she called as the five exited the car. "I thought you might like a snack."

Dom spotted the pink bakery box in her delicate hands. "Let me guess," he smiled.

She pulled back the lid to reveal a pile of apple fritters. "Still hot," she said, offering them to the group. After introductions, they walked toward the buildings. Two were side by side, separated by a strip of overgrown grass. The other sat at a right angle to the farther structure. Each was the size of a two-car garage, with a rolling door in front and a regular, windowed door on the side. Arches decorated each building's front facade. A street ran behind them, parallel to Bel Monte, funneling into a four-way stop that led drivers up the hill to Lions Peak Lane.

"So why did you want us to meet you here?" Dom asked.

"You said that Dion's autopsy indicated that he'd been found across the street, beneath that oak," she began. They all turned as she pointed out the tree, standing by itself at the end of a long, empty field. "And that he had a scrap of paper in his pocket that said BM/C."

Pauly stared blankly.

"Bel Monte and Collina," Dom said slowly, as he read the street signs.

"Right. Well, look around. There's nothing on this corner except these buildings, which don't even have an address. There's a feed lot across the street, but that's farther down."

"And why not use the name of the feed lot instead of cross-streets," Pauly figured aloud.

"Exactly," Giuseppina said. "But that's not all. Didn't you say he had a wound to the back of his head, as well as his forehead? Now, look at that tree. It's far from the road, but still out in the open. Hard to believe no one would've seen whatever happened."

Dom turned back toward the gray buildings. "So, you think somebody whacked him here, and then moved him down there?"

Giuseppina nodded. "Seems like a possibility."

"Or maybe something happened, he wound up dead—unexpectedly—and they had to get rid of him," Dom supposed.

Pauly approached the first building, brushed away a cobweb and peered through the glass in the door. "This one's empty," he said.

"So's this one," called Margaret, looking through a pollen-coated pane of the building closest to Bel Monte.

"But check this out," said Millie from the building in the back. She tried the door handle, but it wouldn't turn. Then she reached into her purse.

"What's that?" Giuseppina asked as Millie pulled out a small pouch.

"My wife has a certain set of *skills*," Pauly proudly announced.

Giuseppina raised a perfectly groomed brow. "How handy."

Within seconds, Millie had popped the lock. Pauly grasped the handle. "Not as much dust and pollen as the other two," he noted. "Tells me it's been used more recently."

Dom stepped inside first and was immediately overcome by the musty odor. "Madonn', that stinks," he said, covering his nose. The others followed him inside, groaning at the stench.

"What is that awful smell?" Giuseppina gasped, raising a linen handkerchief to her nose.

"Blood," the quintet answered in unison, each familiar with the unpleasant scent.

Dom crossed the concrete to inspect a row of shelves that spanned one long wall. They held a variety of trowels, spades, and gloves. A few bags of potting mix, unopened, sat nearby, behind a pair of glossy rubber gardening boots, lit by a sunbeam. Dom crouched to the floor. It was splattered with dark spots, and one long trail that led to the roll-up door. Just beneath the shelves, something small and shiny glinted in the glass-bent rays of the sun.

"Something definitely happened here," he said, noting the dark stains on the concrete. "If you're gonna whack someone, this seems like a good place. Just enough room to move around. Well-lit during the day. And completely concealed. Do your assignment and leave the stiff. Or bring it with you after the fact. Either way, no one's gonna see what you did."

"Hello?" called a voice behind him. "Giuseppina," said a man in a fedora from the doorway, "I saw your car and wanted to make sure you were okay. What are you doing here?"

"Oh, Eufrasio," she replied, "how lovely to see you. We're, uh …"

Her face went blank, and Dom stood up. He recognized the man from the gala and was certain he'd been at the café with his friends the morning Giuseppina paid for the donuts.

"We're trying to find out what happened to a friend," Dom said, walking toward the man and extending his hand. "My name's Dom."

"Eufrasio," the man said, shaking his hand. Then he tipped his fedora to the triplets, pausing momentarily as if he thought he might recognize them. "Who's your friend?"

"My ex-wife's friend, to be specific," Dom clarified. "His name was Dion Maggioli."

Eufrasio's face fell. "Oh, that poor young man," he said. "I'm sorry for your loss. He was a kind soul. But why would you look here?"

Dom turned to Giuseppina, who nodded in encouragement. "Well," he began, "I don't think this is public knowledge yet, but his body was found just across the road."

"*Stai scherzando?* I live right up the hill. I had no idea."

"Eufrasio," Giuseppina said, "do you recall any odd activity here, say, a few weeks ago?"

He thought for a moment. "Not that I can—wait, did you say a few weeks ago?"

"Yes," Dom said. "We're not sure when he died, but he was found on the twenty-third."

"Oh, my anniversary," Eufrasio remarked wistfully. "Georgette and I would've been married fifty-eight years."

An awkward silence filled the space. "What did you do to celebrate?" Giuseppina asked gently. Dom was struck by her graciousness in seemingly any situation.

Eufrasio used a handkerchief to wipe his forehead. "I sat under the madrone. You know that little table by the bocce pit?"

"Antonio and I spent many pleasant hours in conversation there with you and Georgette."

"She loved that spot. In fact, she asked me to plant the madrone there so we could enjoy the shade. I sat and just listened to the air." He dabbed his eyes and folded the handkerchief, tucking it in his pocket. "Sometimes I like to sit outside and think of her."

Giuseppina clasped her hand over his arm. "I understand," she said.

"Anyway," he said, trying to smile, "I was sitting out there that afternoon, and I noticed that a tomato truck pulled up in front of this place. I thought, 'Is this guy lost?' I see tomato trucks all the time. They take Bel Monte so they don't have to use the freeway. But they're not going to get up the hill. The road is too steep and winding."

"Is that all you saw?" Pauly asked.

"There were some other cars," Eufrasio recalled. "I thought it was odd because these buildings have been here for a while, empty. Our homeowner's association has tried to get them torn down, but the city won't do it. No one ever parks here unless they're lost and looking for directions. Maybe someone pulling over to make a phone call."

Susan moved over to the shelves to get a closer look at the cement floor. Then she squatted down and pulled something out from beneath the shelves.

"What kind of cars, do you remember?" Dom asked.

"One was a classic muscle car. Green. Ford. You know, with the stripe and the letters and numbers along the side."

"A Shelby?" Pauly guessed.

Eufrasio tilted his head as he thought. "That sounds right. But it wasn't there the whole time. I saw a man walk over to it. Moved slow."

"Older man?"

"I'd say so. Hard to be sure. He had his back to me, and I was on my terrace. My eyes aren't what they used to be. Reminded me of Laz's brother, though. That walk." He rocked side to side. "Anyway, he stood there for a few minutes, then got in. Kept killing the engine."

"Interesting," Dom said, his mind calculating. "How about the other cars?"

"Oh, one was one of those, oh, what do you call them?" Eufrasio searched for the word. "You know, that guy who builds those electric cars? He wants to go to space?"

"A Tesla," Dom guessed.

"Is that what they're called?" Eufrasio asked. "They're kind of ugly, if you ask me. But I suppose they're fancy. All the young whiz kids down here seem to have them."

Dom looked at Pauly. "What color Tesla?"

"Oh, kind of a dark silver," Eufrasio said. "Very nice."

"Did you see the driver?" Pauly asked.

Eufrasio shook his head. "Not very well," he said. "But she was in a hurry."

Dom ran the information through his mind. "A woman? Older? Younger?"

Eufrasio shrugged. "I can't say. She walked from the door to her car and then sped off."

"Any other cars?" Dom asked.

"Just the tomato truck." He paused, then added, "Come to think of it, you know, I always call them tomato trucks. But they can haul anything. Anyway, it was empty."

"And I wonder how this got here," Susan said, holding the shiny object she'd taken off the floor. It was several links of chain, maybe four inches in total, open at each end.

"That looks like—" Pauly began.

"Dion's chain, from the gala," Dom finished, taking it inspecting it. "Turkish rope."

"What makes you so sure?" Giuseppina asked.

"Oh, Pauly and me, we used to work with, uh, jewelers, occasionally. You know, redistributing inventory. So, I'm familiar with certain types of chains," Dom explained.

As they crowded around Dom to take a look, Millie tripped over the large boots. Pauly caught her, but the boots flipped over, revealing a thick coating of dried mud on the soles.

Margaret held one up. SIZE 12 read the sole. "Look at this," she said. "How much you want to bet the mud on these matches the mud by the tree?"

"But how could we prove that?" Millie asked.

"No one has had access to these buildings for years," Eufrasio said. "Those boots look new. If they'd been left here, they would've been faded and cracked. Believe me, I worked the land for many years and wore through a lot of boots. The sun destroys them."

"Sounds like we might be closer to finding out what happened," Giuseppina said.

Margaret carefully set the boots down. "You think we should call the police?"

Dom, Pauly, Giuseppina, and Eufrasio all chuckled. "I don't know that I'd—" Giuseppina began.

Eufrasio waved his hand. "I think Chief Novak is satisfied that he has his man," he said.

Dom turned to him. "Eufrasio, do you think Carlo did it?"

The old man shook his head. "I would be surprised if he did. To be honest, I don't think he'd have it in him. Don't get me wrong. Carlo Maggioli is—how should I say—not the most stable man in the world. But to murder his own son? And his only heir—"

Giuseppina cleared her throat. Dom picked up the cue.

"Let's say there's a chance Dion wasn't his only heir," Dom posed.

Eufrasio shook his head. "I don't know anything about that. But even if that were true, I can't think of any reason he would want Dion dead. It doesn't make sense. He and Gloria loved that boy. Sure, they had their problems. Every family does. But Carlo was so proud of Dion."

"So why was he arrested?" Margaret asked. "They must have had something on him."

Eufrasio took off his fedora and scratched at the tuft of white hair that crowned his head like a laurel wreath. "I guess leaving the country right after your son's unsolved murder doesn't look so good, especially when you have a history of outbursts and questionable behavior," he said. "But I'm just a *contadino anziani,* so what do I know about these things?"

"An old farmer," Dom said, translating for the triplets. Then he extended his hand to Eufrasio. "Old farmers tend to be wise, *Signore.* You have my respect."

The two shook hands. "I hope you find out what happened to him," Eufrasio said, maintaining a firmer grasp than Dom expected. "He deserves that. Now, I'm off to the market. I'm making Bolognese for dinner with friends this evening and I need to get it started soon." At the door, he turned. "Lucky," he said, snapping his withered fingers and pointing at Susan. "I knew you looked familiar."

"Send him my regards," she said.

"Maybe you should join us for dinner?" he said with a sweet smile.

"Oh, I—" Susan stammered. "Maybe another time."

Eufrasio shrugged. "Suit yourself," he said. Then he tipped his fedora and left.

"Way to blow it, Susie," Margaret chided. "What's wrong with you?"

Giuseppina laughed. "Fortunato Giardi? He's a catch," she said. "But he can be awfully flirtatious. Good heart, though. Well, except for that bypass a few years ago."

The group burst into laughter. "I'll keep that in mind," Susan said. "Thanks."

When the chuckling subsided, Dom asked, "So, what do we do now?"

"Find out who wore those boots," Margaret offered. "Looks like they had a big foot."

"So, a large guy," Susan stated. "Really narrows it down."

"But that means it wasn't Carlo," Giuseppina said. "He's fairly slight."

Margaret picked up the boots. "What are you doing?" Susan said. "That's evidence."

"Look at this," Margaret said. "The mud doesn't go all the way to the toes."

"So?" Millie said.

"Maybe the person who wore these boots had a smaller foot," Margaret supposed.

"So maybe it *was* Carlo," Millie said.

Dom's gut tightened. "I dunno," he said. "Like Eufrasio said, it just don't make sense."

"For what it's worth," Giuseppina offered, "I don't think he did it. I know the family and Eufrasio's right. Carlo loved Dion. He really wanted him to carry on the family name and succeed where Carlo couldn't."

"Speaking of family, did he say Laz's brother? You think he did it?"

"Oh, goodness, no. Ubaldo wouldn't hurt a soul. He's a sweet, kind man. Do you remember him from the gala? Chavonne helped him with the baskets."

"Oh, yeah," Dom said. "He's a little..."

"Unique," Giuseppina smiled, offering Dom a tactful out. "And, I don't know why but this just occurred to me. My husband, Antonio, was an attorney, specializing in wills and trusts. I probably shouldn't tell you this, but there's a clause in Carlo's will that stipulates that his inheritance is passed on to his children if he dies or if he's incarcerated."

"Incarcerated, you say?" Pauly asked. "People think to put that in wills?"

"Yes, but honestly, I can't imagine any reason he'd want to kill his own son."

Dom pulled the chain fragment from his pocket and stared at it. Where it had broken away, the links were warped and rough. He ran his fingers over it. "I guess we're still stuck."

"But we'll get some answers soon," Pauly added.

Hollow consolation. Dom frowned and returned the chain to his pocket.

* * *

With large, knobby hands, Ubaldo Occhipinti slid open his mahogany leather valet. He ran his thick fingers over the row of cufflinks and selected a pair with onyx stones and gold filigree. With age, his fingers had begun to tremble, and it was getting more difficult to fasten his cufflinks. But he had no intention of asking for help. His mother had always insisted he do everything for himself. No accommodations were to be made on his behalf. He attended school, worked the fields, learned to waltz, and became an expert at gin rummy. He'd been taught to drive a tractor, but after he got distracted looking at cloud formations and ran the tractor into a ditch, it was decided that he wouldn't get a driver's license.

Lazaro, however, saw to it that his older brother was protected. Kids could be cruel, hurling terrible insults at Ubaldo, who rarely let words affect him. But Lazaro took it personally. One day in high school, a senior wide receiver named Alan Brantley confronted Ubaldo.

"What's your problem, retard?" the kid taunted. "I saw you lookin' at my girl."

His girl was Joan Keating, who sat across from Ubaldo in biology. She'd left her binder behind and Ubaldo had just returned it to her. When she thanked him, Ubaldo got nervous and had trouble forming the words, "You're welcome." Joan politely waited, encouraging him to finish. But Alan flew into a rage, grabbing him by the collar and shoving him against the bricks.

"Stay away from my girl, Tard," Alan warned, pushing his face into Ubaldo's.

Ubaldo's soft brown eyes looked away, not wanting any trouble. Joan pleaded for Alan to stop, but before she could talk any sense into him, Lazaro appeared. With a piece of metal pipe from shop class concealed in his fist, Lazaro leveled Alan with a single punch. As he groaned on the ground, Lazaro stomped his right foot on the concrete, an inch from Alan's ear.

"Don't ever call him that, prick," Lazaro said, his left foot landing by the other ear.

The wide receiver winced. But he hadn't learned his lesson yet. His face framed by Lazaro's sneakers, he said, "You and that tard gonna do something about it?"

Lazaro dropped his knees onto Alan's chest, pressing hard until he heard gurgling.

"Keep talking, shit for brains, and I will fuck you up," he cautioned, leaning hard on the young man's chest. "You do not want to mess with my family."

With halting breaths, Alan scoffed, "Filthy immigrants who take our land. I ain't afraid."

Lazaro produced the pipe and teasingly ran it down Alan's ribs, as if playing a xylophone. Then he wedged it between two ribs and poked it into the space as far as he could reach. "You sure about that, bitch?" He worked the pipe back and forth in rhythm, violating Alan's ribs in a manner usually reserved for the back seat of a car. "I swear to God, if you ever look at my brother again, I will use this somewhere else and leave it there. You got it?"

Coughing, Alan finally relented. "Okay, okay," he said, prompting Lazaro to stand.

Joan covered her mouth, horrified by what she'd seen. A girlfriend led her away. Meanwhile, Ubaldo quietly observed. When Alan finally rose, he looked small and weak, still coughing as he walked off. Lazaro tucked the pipe into his jacket and motioned to Ubaldo.

"Let's go," he said. They walked home and never said a word about it.

It didn't matter which names the doctors gave Ubaldo's condition. Nothing could change it. "God made you this way," his mother advised. "And if God made you this way, there's nothing wrong with you." Even when he struggled, he believed her. And he knew he was loved.

His folded back his sleeve and threaded the cufflink through the buttonhole. With trembling fingers, he grasped the toggle and tightened it. He needed several tries to fasten the cufflink on his other sleeve. When it was secure, he reached into his valet again. Lifting the tray, he found the silver St. Christopher medal. He ran his hand over the inscription, Dion Ignazio Maggioli. Then he sunk it into his pocket, along with his money clip, and slid the drawer closed.

| 18 |

In her studio, Kate Kendall pored over her notes, sorting and stacking to be sure it was all in order. Peaches meowed and rubbed her head on Kate's pant leg. But Kate was too engrossed in her work to notice it was feeding time. She grabbed a stack of index cards and started jotting. "Dion was last seen on the twenty-third, at the compassion center on Central Road. Marisol said he came by in the morning to drop off groceries and several bouquets of flowers."

She wrote that information on a card, then picked up a new one, writing as she spoke.

"The police report says he was found that afternoon, beneath the oak tree in the field." She laid the card next to the first, creating a timeline. "Carlo, then Ignazio, made monthly payments to Belinda Smith through Figlio Segreto, starting about twenty-five years ago."

Peaches purred and kneaded her claws into the rug at Kate's feet.

"Figlio Segreto means Secret Son," Kate said, underlining the words on the card, then setting alongside the others. "Which explains why Carlo left the company. And according to my FOIA request, the owner of Figlio Segreto is Lazaro Occhipinti."

Kate set the index card on the desk. "So, Lazaro knows Carlo's secret, and he's blackmailing him to keep it quiet." She picked up a new card. "Now, according to the autopsy, Dion had injuries to the front and back of his head," she wrote. "So, it wasn't an accident."

Kate placed the card on the desk and studied the arrangement. "Also," she said, writing out a new card, "if something happens to Carlo, the deeds say that his holdings transfer to his offspring. And if Dion is dead, that leaves—"

Peaches jumped onto the desk with a loud, throttle-like purr, scattering Kate's cards to the floor. She pawed at Kate's pen, then pushed it off the desk's edge. Kate looked at the clock.

"I get it. You're hungry," she said, realizing how late it was. "I'm sorry."

She got up and opened a can of cat food, then plopped it into Peaches' dish. As soon as she set it on the floor, Peaches began eating. Kate washed her hands and then opened the refrigerator. A jar of mayonnaise, three expired yogurts, a dozen diet sodas, and a withering cucumber were the highlights. She closed the door, then grabbed her purse. "Lasagna it is," she announced to Peaches, who was still wolfing down her food.

***

Dom let his stomach growl as he sat on his bed, gazing out the window. He always felt uneasy the night before a job and found it hard to eat.

"The gals picked up Chinese food," Pauly said, popping his head into Dom's room. "They got those dumplings you like. Come and eat."

"I'm not hungry. Think I'll stay in here a while."

Pauly watched his friend, familiar with this behavior and knowing better than to try to change his mind. "We'll have leftovers," he said. "Take your time."

Dom pulled the letter and his phone from his nightstand. He stared at Florence's number, ready to dial. Instead, he sent a text. "Can I call?"

A few minutes went by before she replied. "Sure."

Dom's stomach clenched tighter. He'd convinced himself that he'd never go back to this life, and vowed he'd change his ways if there were any chance of getting back with Florence. And now he had to tell her that there would be yet one more job. With a deep exhale, he dialed.

"Hello," came the raspy response on the other end.

"Flo? Oh, it didn't sound like you."

"It's me," she said softly over a hum in the background.

"Sorry," he said. "I know it's late, but I wanted to talk to you about Dion. And, about us."

He waited for her answer, which came slowly after a short coughing burst. Dom figured she was preparing herself for the worst. "Go ahead."

Dom tried to find the gentlest way to tell her. "I think we're gonna get information tomorrow," he said. "The cops arrested Carlo, but I gotta be honest. I don't think he did it."

He could hear Florence inhale deeply. "Oh?" she said, barely above a whisper.

"It's upsetting, I know," he said. "But somethin' about this ain't right, y'know? My gut's in knots." He thought giving more details about the job they were scheduled to do but knew it would upset her. "Anyway," he said, glossing it over, "gonna see what we can find out."

Florence exhaled. "Good," she said. "What else?"

Dom looked at the letter. *Here goes nothing.*

"Flo, I wrote something down," he began. "You know how I get, always forgetting stuff and twisting it around, getting mixed up in the middle. Remember at our wedding? I kept saying Florence Louisiana, not Florence Luisa Anna, when we took our vows. Madonn', I'm glad Pauly made me say it right. I might-a wound up married to a state in the south."

A weak chuckle ending in a coughing fit came from the other end of the line. "I remember," she said, and Dom could hear the smile in her voice.

"You need some water?" Dom asked.

She cleared her throat and inhaled deeply. "No, go ahead."

"You sound tired," Dom noted.

"Go on," she urged.

"All right," he said, the letter shaking in his hand. His knotted stomach tightened as he read the part about being the villain in someone else's story. It razed him that he'd written those words with good intentions but decided to go back to his old lifestyle before she heard them.

"Florence, I don't expect that you can forgive me, but seeing what happened to Dion has made me realize how short and how precious life is," he said, drawing to the end of the letter. "If there's any chance for me to come back into your life, I'd like to try. I promise I will spend whatever time we have left doing what I should have done from the start.

"Loving you. Cherishing you. And taking care of you."

He suddenly realized he hadn't finished writing the letter, and he didn't know what to say next. His phone trembled in his hand, waiting for her answer. "Florence?"

* * *

Eufrasio sat up in his chair and checked his phone when he heard the alert that sounded like a cello. One notification from his calendar app.

Dominoes tomorrow afternoon at Miliani's.

Bartolomeo, Eight Ball, and Lucky would all be there, as they were every other Thursday. They'd sit at the horseshoe-shaped bar for a cocktail first, then move to a table for their game. Eight Ball brought the dominoes. The restaurant staff knew to deliver a pot of coffee and four slices of cake after about an hour. With gnarled hands, they gripped the smooth pieces that had eroded with time's passing. On some, the pips had worn off, but the men still knew their value. It was those dominoes that most reminded Eufrasio of their friendship. Familiar, comfortable, a little worse for the wear. But still capable of providing entertainment.

The breeze rustled through the madrone, sweeping into the open window like the flick of a fringed shawl. At this time of year, the evening air was richly scented with garlic, either from crops or cooking. Tonight was no exception. It was golden hour, when the sun gets broad as it squats along the horizon, ushering in the night. The warm light filtered through the windows, casting comforting beams along Eufrasio's bookcases. This was when the sun illuminated the large photo of his darling Georgette. Taken outside their wedding chapel, the sepia-toned picture showed her gown fanned out, the train embroidered by hand with the flowers of their ancestral Calabria. Her gown was as pale and regal as the cliffs that met the Ionian Sea. Her smile as pleasant as the Mediterranean breeze rippling over azure waves. Eufrasio waited in his chair each night for the warm glow to bring her back to life. He set down his phone and took her in.

* * *

"You want the last dumplings?" Margaret asked Susan, boxing up leftovers.

"Oh, save those for Dom," Pauly said. "They're his favorite." Margaret shrugged and pushed the cartons onto the shelf. "So, what are you ladies doing tomorrow?" Pauly asked as he doled out fortune cookies.

"Not sure," Susan said, passing Millie plates for the dishwasher. "Maybe just stay here?"

"Sounds like a plan," Pauly said, cracking open his cookie.

Susan read her fortune. "You will fall into the arms of a handsome stranger."

"Let me see," Margaret pleaded, grabbing the fortune. "Wow, it really says that!"

"That decides it," Millie said. "We gotta make sure Susan has a chance to get lucky."

Millie and Margaret laughed. "Malarkey," Susan said, rolling her eyes.

"Come on, Susie," Margaret said, "don't be a stick in the mud. We'll go to lunch."

"Oh, I know," Millie said. "How about Miliani's? I hear it's haunted. Let's check it out."

"Bet it's full of eligible bachelors," Margaret quipped.

"You mean ghosts or actual, living men?" Millie cackled.

Susan flicked the dish towel at them. "Shut up," she said sternly, then broke out laughing as she chased after them. Pauly pulled the fortune from his cookie.

As secrets are revealed, so is danger. Use caution.

"Honey, what's yours say?" Millie asked, breathlessly sidling up to her husband.

Pauly tore the fortune in half and then crumpled it into the garbage. "Something stupid," he said. "Come on, let's watch TV in our room."

* * *

"Florence?" Dom repeated. "Are you there?"

"Dom-i-nic," she said, drawing out his name, "I'm here. And I want you to know I've waited such a long time to hear you say those words."

Dom's pulse flickered. Even knowing what he was about to do tomorrow, he was at ease knowing Florence was happy. "I'm sorry it took so long," he said. "Florence—"

"Dom," she said, "I don't have much time. Please just let me say this."

He watched the sun fade over the foothills as she spoke.

Florence slowly ran her withered fingers over the brooch Dom had sent her after their score in Seattle. She'd worn it on her robe every day since she'd moved to this place. "I know it wasn't easy for you to do what you did, to walk away from that life. I wouldn't blame you if you wanted to go back. I think it's all you've ever known. But I also want you to know how much I appreciate you going to find out what happened to Dion. Whatever you learn tomorrow, it means the world to me. I've always known that you loved me. That you didn't want it to end. And how much it hurt when I walked away. I'm sorry for the pain I caused you."

Dom's throat bulged. How could she apologize to him after all he'd put her through?

"Flo, I—"

"Shh," she said, her voice thinner now. "I told you, I don't have much time. I had to look out for myself. But I want you to know, I never stopped loving you. Yes, we divorced. And yes, I remarried. And Rafael was a wonderful man. But he could never take your place."

Tears welled in Dom's eyes. Had he heard her correctly? Was this really happening?

"Dominic, you're not the bad guy you think you are. You're no choir boy. But you're not a villain. Not in my story, anyway."

"Oh, Flo," he said, unable to wait any longer, "it's so good to hear you say that."

"And I want you to know that I forgive you, darling," she said. "I forgive you, and I will always love you. But…" A rattling cough resonated from the line. "It's too late for us."

"Flo, don't say that."

She cleared her throat, her voice raspy and weak. "But I want you to move on. Don't wait to do what makes you happy. Don't put your life on hold. Live it while you still can, *mio caro*."

Dom waited, trying not to interrupt again. But the line was silent, except for a series of beeps and then a long, even mechanical tone. "Flo? Florence, are you there?"

Another voice came on the phone. "Sir, this is Nancy. I'm a nurse at the hospice center. Your wife has been here for a few weeks. She had lung cancer and didn't want you to know. But she was very clear that she wanted to talk to you before she…"

Dom didn't even hear the rest. The knot in his stomach swelled to a boulder, pressing against his other internal organs. His breath froze, a tight belt of dread constricting his lungs. Sweat showered him as he pressed his face into his pillows and let out a deep, gasping wail.

| 19 |

He hadn't even heard Pauly knock or open the bedroom door. The angular rooftops set against the sloping foothills were his only focus.

"Dom," Pauly repeated from the dimly lit doorway, "what is it?"

The sunlight had been extinguished now. Evaporated in a moment's time, just as he had begun to appreciate it. Only a faint blue glimmer of twilight remained.

"She's gone," Dom said, his throat jagged with emotion.

"Who's gone? What are you talking about?"

He stared at a spot on the dusky horizon, centering on a faraway flicker where the pale moonlight reflected from the glass of a lofty estate. "Florence," Dom said. "She's…"

He couldn't bring himself to say it. The words were bitter in his mouth. The taste of hope destroyed. Everything he wanted taken away instantaneously. Irreparably. And nothing—no heroic deed, no amount of money, nothing—would bring it back.

Pauly sat down on the bed. "How?"

Dom's chest loosened, just enough for him to speak. "She knew it all along," he said. "All those times she told me she couldn't talk? What she meant was she *literally* couldn't talk. I guess all those years of smoking finally caught up to her. She was on oxygen, being treated for lung cancer. In hospice. I spoke with her tonight and that was it."

"Aww, I'm sorry," Pauly said, laying a hand on Dom's shoulder. "But I'm glad you got to talk to her, finally."

His cheek already damp, Dom let his tears stream unrestricted. "And do you know what she said? My sweet Florence? She said that she forgave me for all I done. And that she never stopped loving me." His voice cracked as the moon's pale beams cast their glow on the rooftops. "And now she's gone."

Pauly put his arms around Dom and let him dissolve. A grown man, who'd beaten, robbed, stolen, and killed without remorse to uphold his loyalty to a lifestyle, now reduced to quivering cries absorbed by the shoulder of his best friend. There was nothing else to say. So, they sat in silence, punctuated by breathy gasps and sniffling sobs, holding onto each other as the moon ascended the horizon.

* * *

When Dom woke up, he was alone. His shoes pulled off, the blanket tucked around his chest. Pauly must have done it, he thought, as he stretched his neck and released a series of cracks and pops. He reached to his nightstand to turn on the lamp. As his meaty hand knocked the letter to the floor, the memory of Florence flooded his mind. A suffocating grief consumed him. But he shoved it aside, as he'd done with other unpleasant thoughts over the years and steeled his resolve. It was not a day to mourn. That could come later. Today was for justice.

* * *

"Good morning," Susan said, handing Dom a cup of coffee. "Pauly told us... I'm sorry."

"Thanks, Susie. I appreciate that."

They sipped their coffee quietly at the dining table, letting the caffeine do its job. The now familiar scent of dew and garlic wafted in from the windows. Dom watched a hummingbird flit outside the window, visiting the trumpet vine that curled up the porch. The opalescent green feathers shone in the early light. He thought about Florence and smiled, grateful she was at rest.

"So, what are your plans today?" he asked.

"Lunch with the girls," Susan replied. "Pauly said you guys have business?"

Dom turned away from the window, unsure of how to answer. "He told you?"

Susan shook her head. "Yeah, after you went to bed," she said. "He told us about Florence. Then he said you're doing something today—a job. Should help you learn what happened to Dion."

Dom stared blankly. "And?"

"And we said that's all we need to know," Susan said. "Look, we might be blonde, but we're not dumb. We know it's dangerous. Do what you gotta do. For Dion. For Florence. We trust you'll be smart and stay safe. But we figured it was best if we don't know too much."

Dom smiled, thinking about Florence giving him the same kind of speech as many times as she did. "Susan, in case I never said it before, you and your sisters are very sharp cookies."

She leaned toward him as if ready to disclose a secret. "I know," she said with a wink, then sipped her coffee. The hummingbird dipped its needle-like beak into a cluster of flowers, draining them one by one. Then it hovered above the vine for a moment and flew away.

* * *

Dom checked his watch. Nearly 9:45. He tapped his fingers on his dresser.

"You know what to do?" Pauly asked from the doorway.

Dom pulled out his Beretta and checked the magazine. Then he felt for the silencer in his pocket. Tucking two more magazines into his pocket, he nodded. "Yep," he said. "Let's go."

They walked outside and turned the corner as instructed. Dom checked his watch. 9:58.

"You know, days like this, I wish I hadn't given up smoking," Pauly quipped.

Dom flinched, thinking about Florence.

"Oh, Dom, that was a dumb thing to say," Pauly offered. "I'm sorry."

"It's all right. But you know, I was thinking. Remember Flo's text. It said, TAKE U FOR A DRIVE."

"Yeah, that didn't make sense to me."

"Remember how Big Mike said he saw Dion's Shelby that day he was at the feed lot?"

"Yeah, so?"

"And then Eufrasio said that the guy who walked to the car reminded him of—"

"Laz's brother."

"Ubaldo," they said together.

"And he kept killing the engine. You think that guy killed Dion, too?" Pauly asked.

But before Dom could reply, a dark sedan pulled up. They knew the drill. Look casual.

The passenger window lowered. An older man ducked his head, peering over sunglasses. "Hey, you fellas new in town?"

Pauly stepped forward, reciting the code he'd rehearsed. "Yeah, we are."

"You thirsty?" the man asked.

"Matter of fact, we are," Dom said, sticking to the script. "You know a good juice bar?"

"It's funny," the man said, "I was just going to get some juice. Hop in."

With a click, the back doors unlocked. They got in, knowing to keep their eyes forward. Yet they'd assessed the wheelman already. Late fifties, regular schmoe, forgettable face. Probably a lifer, just like them. And, surely, well-armed.

"So," the man said, surprising them as they passed the block with the police station, "are you ready for an adventure?"

This wasn't part of the plan. Dom felt Pauly's eyes glance his way, panicked. Calmly, Dom watched Craftsman cottages and stately Victorians morph into rows of cookie cutter homes. "We're ready for anything," he said confidently. Pauly's shoulders eased.

"Good," the man said, taking a side street. "You look like guys who enjoy adventure."

"We enjoy many things," Dom said, calculating his risk. "Tasteful jewelry. A plate of antipasti. Maria Callas arias. A nice dry Tempranillo. Sending messages to rats who need to be reminded of where their loyalty lies. And the means to afford the finer things in life."

"Then I think our interests are in alignment and this relationship can be mutually beneficial," the driver said. "Maybe extended after this, if you're looking for more experience."

"We got plenty of experience," Dom said dryly.

"So I hear," the driver replied. "Staten Island? I could tell from your voices."

Dom nodded, aware that an answer was expected, but unsure of what to say. Suddenly he began to wonder if there was a connection to Sal Alimonto or another "colleague" they'd missed. So, he zipped his lip and watched the scenery.

The driver proceeded toward Central Road, turning down every other street, driving for a block, and then turning north. Dom and Pauly knew what he was doing, creating a jagged pattern that would be harder for witnesses to recreate.

"Been doin' this a while?" Pauly asked.

The man glanced at them from the rearview mirror as he threaded the sedan through a narrow tree-lined street. "A while," he said.

Pauly's shoulders crept upward again.

Message received.

"When our associates are in place, I'll drop you off in the alley near your work sites. You take those briefcases on the floor," the man instructed. "Each one has two bags inside. When you collect the juice, it goes in those bags. Then the bags go back in the briefcases. You will have ten minutes to complete your job. I will be parked at the train depot up the block. You find me and get in the car. Then I'll take you to the drop. You understand your assignments?"

"I got the pet store," Dom said.

"And I got the bowling alley," Pauly replied.

"Our associates have the pawn shop, the bridal boutique, and the travel office," the man explained. "Those are all within two blocks.

Everything is timed so that you will finish simultaneously. But there's no room for error. You get your job done and get back to the car. The others have their own transportation and will meet us at the drop. Got it?"

"Got it," Dom and Pauly answered in unison.

A muted buzz came from the front seat and the driver looked over at his phone, mounted on the dash. "All right," he said, steering the sedan into an alley. "It's time."

* * *

Kate Kendall took a swig of her diet soda, then let out a low burp. Peaches scratched at her post and flicked her tail. Kate dealt her index cards onto the desk like a hand of Solitaire. She studied them carefully as she nursed her drink, revising the order until she was satisfied. All the puzzle pieces finally fit together. She clicked open a pen and numbered the cards. Then she stacked them again and secured them with a binder clip before tucking them into her messenger bag. A quick shower and she'd be ready to go to the office to file this bombshell of a story.

* * *

Gloria Maggioli admired the pair of silver candlesticks she'd placed on the mantel. A gift from an old friend from Staten Island, packed away after Carlo said they looked tacky. She wished she'd stood up to him when he said Florence's thoughtful gesture didn't fit their décor. But he was locked up now and couldn't give his opinion on the things that pleased her.

Florence had been kind enough to send Dion a birthday card, with a $10 bill tucked inside, every year. And he thoughtfully sent thank you notes and told her about his endeavors. But Carlo had discouraged her from contacting Florence or anyone from her old neighborhood. Now that she was liberated from his watchful eyes, Gloria wondered how Florence might be doing. Maybe she'd try to contact her after lunch.

She leaned on her cane and sipped her gin, enjoying the way the candlesticks gleamed in the late morning light, and her newfound freedom.

* * *

Carlo idled in his windowless cell. His hair, stringy and greasy after refusing to bathe for days, clung to the shoulders of his orange jumpsuit. He stared at the floor, eyes sunken and shadowed from a lack of sleep. It awed him that anyone could believe that he'd kill his own son. But he was beyond emotion at this point. Beyond rage. Beyond grief. Not only was Dion dead, but his biggest fear was about to come true. Those loans were due next week. A huge balloon payment he'd gambled on decades ago, his cockiness convincing him the impossible was indeed possible. Literally letting his mouth—and his ego—write a check his arrogant ass couldn't cash. And now, sitting in jail with no means to collect, his life might as well be over.

* * *

"Not now, Princess," Lazaro said into his phone as he drove toward San Jose.

"But Daddy," Chavonne protested, "I need to talk to you about the profit-loss statement that comes out next week. Have you seen these numbers?"

"Sweetheart," he said, weaving his Alfa Romeo Spider through traffic on Highway 85 like a crimson-checkered serpent hunting rodents in a cornfield. "I'm picking up your mother's birthday gift at the jewelers. Then I have to get back down there for a meeting."

"I know," she said. 'I have the same meeting, remember? The investors will hammer us."

"I wouldn't worry about it too much," Lazaro said, throttling the Spider to zip past an elderly lady in an Oldsmobile, emitting a lusty roar.

"Dad," Chavonne said soberly, "we're short on cash. The gala didn't bring in the profits we anticipated, thanks to that incident during the auction. And I'm a little worried that we—"

"Honey," Lazaro said, "it'll be taken care of. I promise. In fact, very soon, we'll have all the cash we need. Besides, has Daddy ever let you down?"

Frustrated, she knew not to dig too deep. Being Lazaro Occhipinti's daughter had its perks. But it came with an understanding that some questions were best left unasked.

"All right," she sighed.

"That's my girl," he said. "Trust me, sweetheart. It's handled. See you at lunch."

Chavonne hung up and fell back on her bed, wondering what her father—and no doubt, her brothers—were up to this time. "All the cash we need" seemed like a cocky boast. She reached into her nightstand for her journal. The rose petals she'd pressed from Dion's final bouquet were nearly dry, and their fragrance sweetened the air as they tumbled onto her duvet.

"Oh Dion," she said, gathering the scattered petals. "Why couldn't you give me what I wanted? It would've been so easy, and it would've changed everything. We could've been free."

* * *

Ubaldo Occhipinti shuffled down the sidewalk with his unsteady gait and ran his thumb over the St. Christopher medal, now a fixture in his pocket. It brought to mind shouts echoing off a cement floor and empty walls. The smell of musty air baked by sunlight. His agreement to do a favor for someone who never needed to ask him for anything. The thrill of unbridled horsepower beneath his right foot. Momentary joy that made him feel like a kid again, tooling through the vineyard on a summer afternoon. No one to call him names or belittle his intellect. Pure freedom.

Touching the thick silver medallion helped him focus. When he stumbled for a word or couldn't sort his thoughts, he concentrated on the varied textures. On one side, the relief of St. Christopher, staff in hand and carrying the infant Christ on his back, was pleasantly bumpy. As he dragged his thumb across it, he felt each groove and protrusion, envisioning the martyr in his mind. The back of the medal was smooth, save for the etched inscription of Dion's name, deeply scratched into the silver disk. But despite its calming effect, this medal bore a terrible secret. A burden Ubaldo had decided he could no longer carry.

* * *

Pauly entered the bowling alley, nearly empty except for a few old men on the far lanes, polishing their balls. He wished Dom was there so he could make a joke, but he knew he had to focus on the job. The manager's office was little more than a closet, just past the unattended counter for collecting fees and renting shoes. The odor of liquefied cheez with a Z emanated from the snack bar. Combined with the polyurethane and disinfectant, it created an unpleasant taste in Pauly's throat. He choked back a gag, then strode into the doorway of the dimly lit space.

"Rentals up front," said the man at the desk, not bothering to look up from his computer.

"Not here to rent," Pauly said, hoisting the briefcase. "Here to collect." The man's stubbled face tensed. Pauly pulled his windbreaker aside, revealing his sidearm.

"Oh," the man said, backing away from the desk. "I didn't know that was today."

"My associates sent a reminder," Pauly said, coldly drawing his fingers across his throat.

The man stood up, sweaty as he caught a bottle of hand sanitizer he'd nearly knocked over. "They did," he said. "I just thought that Carlo, er, I mean, I thought I had until next week."

"This is not something that gets rescheduled to your convenience," Pauly said, putting a hand on his piece as he leaned into the doorway.

"It's in my safe," the man said, pulling up raggedy carpet. "I just didn't know it was—"

"Get the juice and quit your yappin'," Pauly said, eyes locked on the man in case he wanted to try something funny. The man pulled a box from the floor and opened it with quivering hands. Once Pauly could see there was no weapon inside, he laid the briefcase on the desk and removed the bags. "Everything in there. Come on," he urged. "Make it fast."

"It's in two piles, fifty grand each," the man said, neatly loading the cash into the bags.

"I don't give a fuck about your COD or whatever it's called," Pauly said, aiming his gun. "Get it in there and shut up before I give this place a stain you can't get out."

The man finished putting the money in the bags. Then Pauly set them in the briefcase and snapped it closed. Now he just had to head to the alley. This was easier than he remembered. But when he turned to leave, he plowed into three white-haired ladies in hot pink satin jackets, the words Silver Strikers emblazoned on the back with glittering rhinestones. One of their bowling bags swung into Pauly, folding him at the waist. His briefcase intertwined with another bag, knotting them together and sending them tumbling to the floor like dice from a Yahtzee cup.

"Oh, my hip!" one of the ladies cried. "I think I broke it."

"Myrtle, you're on my leg," yelled another. "Get off me, you heifer."

Pauly was stuck at the bottom of the pile, which looked like a game of Twister gone bad at the nursing home. He desperately tried to extract his limbs from the tangled mess but didn't want to let go of the briefcase. An orthopedic-shoed foot had pinned his wrist to the floor.

"Damn it, Clara, move your ass," snapped the third lady.

"My hip!" cried the first.

Pauly jerked his arm free, upending the pile again as he scrambled to his feet. While the women moaned and groaned, he slipped outside.

His pulse racing, he did his best to maintain a quick but unsuspicious pace as he headed to the meeting spot.

＊＊＊

The pet store's turtle tank greeted Dom as he entered. The amphibians crawled over each other, piling up to reach the upper edge. They craned their wrinkly necks over the side, only to slip back into the shallow, murky water below and start over. Dom's eyes scanned the stacks of dog food, heaped on wire shelves. He passed a row of rat cages, packages of cat toys, and a spinning rack of leashes and collars. Then he proceeded to the counter in the back.

"Can I help you?" came a friendly, feminine voice.

Madonn', why did it have to be a woman?

"Here for a pickup," he said as a young lady hopped off a stool behind the cash register.

"A pickup?" she asked, her blonde ponytail tilting to one side. "For what?"

Dom shifted his weight, unsure of how to proceed. "Uh, you the owner?"

"Nah, my dad," she said, flashing her braces. "I'm just watching the shop while he's out."

Shit.

"Will he be back soon?"

She shrugged. "He didn't say."

"Uh," Dom said, stressing, "did he say he had anything to give anyone? A package?"

She shook her head. "Nope. Don't think so."

Dom's eyes drifted to the clock behind her. His gut filled with dread as he watched the second hand tick-tick-tick in a circle.

Now what?

"Kassidy," called a voice from the back, "I'm back."

Thank God.

A man appeared, lugging a toolbox. He set it on the counter with a clank. "Hi."

"Here for a pickup," Dom said, not wanting to waste time with pleasantries.

"Oh," the man said, his smile dissolving. He reached into his front pocket for a stack of bills. "Kass, go to the coffee place and get me a mocha and a muffin, and whatever you want."

"Can I get ice cream?"

"Sure," the man said, his eyes locked with Dom's.

"And a milkshake? No, wait, a brownie sundae?"

"Whatever you want," the man said. "Just go."

She snatched the bills and shoved them in her pocket. "Thanks!" she squealed as she left.

"Sorry," the man said. "I didn't know you were coming today. I mean, with Carlo in—"

"Yeah, well I'm here now," Dom said, "so let's go."

"It's in here," the man said, motioning to a locked file cabinet behind the counter. He fumbled with a set of keys. As he slipped one and then another into the lock, Dom watched the seconds tick-tick-tick again. Finally, he opened the drawer and Dom reached for the briefcase.

"For what it's worth," the man began, "I don't think Carlo killed his son."

Dom slid the briefcase across the counter and hold out the bags. "You don't?"

Filling the bags, the man said, "No. Carlo's—look, you know. You work for him. He's an *interesting* guy. I just don't think he's a murderer. But I guess we all have secrets, rights?"

Tick-tick-tick.

Dom suddenly remembered why he was there. And that between the wait and his bad knees and back, he'd be cutting it close to get to the meeting spot. "Secrets. Right," he said. "But I don't got time to chit-chat. That everything?"

The man watched the door. "A hundred thousand, as requested. Just, please, do me a favor," he said. "My daughter—"

Dom snapped the briefcase closed. "Don't worry. I ain't gonna hurt no kid."

"Thank you," the man said. "Again, I'm sorry for the delay."

Dom grabbed the briefcase and started toward the door. When it swung open, a woman holding a long pink leash strolled in. At the end of the leash was a spry Yorkshire terrier. It yapped and growled, straining to reach Dom's ankles. He froze.

"Oh, Pixie, behave yourself," the woman said, yanking the leash.

Dom flashed back to that tragic day in Seattle, and his stomach tightened all over again. Snapping at his pant legs, the Yorkie growled louder.

"I'm sorry," the woman said. "I think that's twice now—"

Dom, aware he was way behind schedule, pushed through the door. As he hustled up the sidewalk, sweat soaked his back. There was noise behind him, but he didn't dare look back. Besides, he was breathing so hard, he could barely hear anything else. Just get to the sedan and then off to the drop.

A faint train whistle echoed as he passed the furniture stores and the medical supply outlet. His knees were aching, but he pushed on. Almost there. When he saw the murals, he turned and hurried toward the depot. A block later, he saw Pauly standing beneath a shade tree, as if waiting for a bus. Dom walked to the far end of the lot, stepped over the train tracks, and crossed the street, not wanting to be seen together. It was bad enough they were carrying matching briefcases. He scanned the parking lot, looking for anyone in a car who might make them. It seemed that they were alone, but he knew not to get too comfortable. The briefcase sagged in his meaty grip, heavy with mixed emotions. Shame. Regret. Grief. All the things he'd sworn to leave behind. It occurred to him that this was both physical and symbolic baggage, and he struggled to hold its weight.

This is definitely the last job. Definitely.

At last, the sedan pulled up near where Pauly was standing. But as Dom started walking toward it, a thunderous rumble filled the air, followed by a loud series of clangs and a piercing whistle.

"Madonn'!" he yelled as he watched the red and white-striped crossing gates descend. He'd been so focused on hurrying to get back to the meeting spot and looking inconspicuous that he didn't realize he was on the other side of the tracks. He looked down the street, thinking he could run across them before it was too late. The sleek silver nose of the train hurtling toward him and the burn in his arthritic knees collaborated to negate that idea. A trio of whistle blasts ripped through the air. There was nothing to do but wait until it passed.

Dom's heart raced as he suddenly felt like a target, like those little mechanical ducks at the fair, waiting to get shot. He was standing helplessly with a briefcase full of juice and nowhere to run. The train began whirring past. He glanced around, always on alert for someone ready to take him out. On the next block, he saw a police cruiser pull to a stop. A fountain of sweat drenched his brow.

Be cool.

He looked back toward the tracks. Clack-clack-clack. The train continued to chug along. He shifted his weight and fidgeted, nearly letting the briefcase slip from his sweaty hand. With a casual glance, he looked over his shoulder to the next block. But the cruiser was gone.

His heart pounded as loud as the passing train now. A deafening thrum that wouldn't quit. Clack-clack-clack. His breath came in jagged jolts, nearly suffocating him, and his stomach clenched into an acidic ball, ready to burst. Dom's knees weakened and he began to totter.

But just as he was sure he would collapse, the caboose passed. As the safety gates began to raise, he hurried to cross the tracks. A slight jog was all he could muster at this point, unable to feel his feet, let alone his legs. Like running in slow motion through a bog of oatmeal. The sedan was waiting, and he hurried to it while being careful to appear nonchalant.

"The fuck," Pauly said, as Dom piled into the back seat next to him.

"I didn't know there'd be a train comin'," Dom said, his breath halting.

"It's my fault for being late," the driver said. "Some old broad broke a hip, and they were loading her into an ambulance up the street. Everything go okay?"

"Yeah," Pauly said, craning his neck to look down the street.

"All good," Dom gulped as his pulse began to recover.

They tooled out of the parking lot and the driver headed south, again taking a jagged route of side streets until he reached his destination. Miliani's Restaurant.

"Here we are, gents," he said. "Go in, sit at the bar. Our associates will be along shortly."

They entered the restaurant, awed by giant panels depicting cowboy scenes over the horseshoe bar. There were several ebony tables with ivory-padded chairs arranged throughout the space. They walked to the bar and were about to sit down when Dom spotted a familiar face.

"Oh shit," he said under his breath. "What's she doin' here?"

"Hm?" Pauly said, turning to see Giuseppina Rosetto perched at the far end of the bar. She was resplendent in a beautiful jade green dress and matching felt hat, glittery jewels adorning the back. This dame knew how to dress. Looking like a 1940s starlet, her fingers were curled around a dirty martini as she enjoyed a joke with four men in fedoras.

* * *

Gloria Maggioli sipped her gin from a table near the back wall of Miliani's, hoping her headache would go away. She stared out the window, watching an ambulance roll by. But the sound of uneven footsteps approaching the table caught her attention.

"Mrs. ... Maggioli," said a deep voice.

Ubaldo Occhipinti loomed over her, resting a large hand on the table. Carlo had warned that Ubaldo was "some kind of perv." And that scared her.

"Yes," she said cautiously.

"May I sit down?" he asked, forming the words carefully as he moved his other hand inside his pocket. "I think I have something ... that ... belongs to you."

* * *

Lazaro Occhipinti breezed into Miliani's, cell phone to his ear. "Not my problem," he snapped as he brushed past a waitress and headed to a table away from the windows. "Do it." He smiled at his daughter, seated among investors, as he slid his phone into his suit pocket.

"Good morning," he said, shaking hands and leaning down to kiss his daughter's cheek before sitting at the head of the table. "How is everyone today?"

"We were just talking about potential real estate acquisitions," Chavonne piped up.

"Is that so?" Lazaro asked.

"Yes, but I explained that we'd need to acquire more capital before we can—"

Lazaro's eyes drifted to the door as Silvestro, Nunzio, and Onorato strolled in, carrying briefcases. Silvestro nodded, but Lazaro gave no response. Instead, he turned to Chavonne and smiled as if telling a child it was too close to dinnertime to have a cookie. "That won't be a problem," he said, then picked up his menu. "I'm starving. Shall we order?"

Chavonne's mouth dropped, but she knew better than to disagree with her father in public. She opened her menu, concealing the seething rage in her face.

Let him play his game.

* * *

Silvestro straddled a bar stool next to Dom as Nunzio wedged in next to Pauly. Onorato stood behind them. "You guys order already?" Silvestro asked.

"I hear the juice is good here," Dom said.

Silvestro put a hand on Dom's shoulder, then Pauly's. "Let's go to the back and discuss this further, shall we?"

Onorato guided them to a small room behind the bar, past the restrooms. With Silvestro's hand still on him, Dom's jacket spread open, revealing the Beretta tucked into his waistband. As they passed Giuseppina, Dom looked away. "Keep moving, old man," Onorato said.

* * *

Kate Kendall came down the stairs and stopped at the door. Did she remember her office keys? Without looking up, she moved aside for a trio of women, letting them pass as she dug inside her messenger bag. Lip balm. Pens. Steno pads. An earring. A flyer for fifteen percent off a spa treatment. *Like I'm gonna use that.* And, her stack of index cards. But no keys. Exasperated, she turned to go back to her studio, her leopard print flats echoing on the stairs.

* * *

"Listen," Susan said, her nose in a book as the triplets entered Miliani's. "Built in the 1920s, Miliani's was a whistle stop on the way to Hollywood. Frequented by stars like Clark Gable and Will Rogers, and noted for its unique western décor, this historic restaurant brings you back to a simpler time. Try the Linguini Miliani, with petite clams draped in velvety garlic sauce, paired with a dirty martini featuring garlic-stuffed olives and bleu cheese. Don't forget the Blackout Chocolate Cake to complete the experience."

"Sold," Millie said, looking for a table. When a hostess approached, Margaret and Millie followed her. Susan, still reading, tripped over a diner's purse, stumbling. Two strong hands steadied her, and she gazed into a pair of deep blue eyes and a gleaming, familiar smile.

"Well," the tanned, elderly gentleman practically purred, "it's your Lucky day at last."

***

Dom looked at the bottles on the shelves in the little room. Grenadine. Tequila. Aperol. And an entire row of seltzer. Pauly sat next to him, and they all put their briefcases on the table.

"Nunzio," Silvestro said, sitting across from Dom and Pauly, "watch the door."

"How come I always—"

A glare from his older brother quieted his protest and he took his post outside. Meanwhile, Onorato smiled confidently, his broad shoulders stretching his well-tailored suit.

"Well, gentleman, we have business to attend," he said, adjusting a cuff and opening Nunzio's briefcase as if performing in a play. He picked up a stack of bills and began counting. "Now, the deal was thirty thousand between the two of you. After a small fee."

"No," Dom said plainly. "That's not what we agreed to. Thirty thousand each, no fee."

Onorato smiled. It was the kind of dimpled grin that made young women forget their standards and fall for a bad boy. He was handsome, but there was a darkness to him.

Dom recalled having that same swagger a few decades ago. And he recognized Onorato's attempt at intimidating them. Pauly was right. These mooks were just younger versions of themselves. Simple aspirations. Trying to get ahead. Using their muscle to persuade others to comply. But he and Pauly had something these young thugs didn't have: experience.

"Well, our terms have changed," Onorato said, his dark eyes flaring. "Take it or leave it."

"No," Dom said, matching Onorato's leveling stare as he laid his hand on the briefcase. Pauly did the same. The young man let the hint of a nervous chuckle escape, then focused.

"I hired you for a job, sort of an audition," he began. "So far, I like what I see. I could keep you busy, and well-compensated even after our cut. For a couple old guys, you did good."

"Old doesn't mean incapable," Pauly said. "You should show some respect."

Silvestro and Onorato broke out laughing. "You're talking to us about respect? On our turf?" Onorato asked as his laughter subsided. "Oh, that's rich. Ain't it, Sly?"

"Rich," Silvestro echoed.

Dom chortled. "Look, fellas, we know your game. Double-dipping while collecting for your old man out there, Lazaro. He owns this whole town. Ain't that right?"

Silvestro stopped laughing and sat up in his chair.

"I bet Daddy's gonna be pissed when he finds out you're screwin' him on the cut," Pauly offered. "Skimmin' right off the top to line your own pockets."

"Oh, but not you, Onorato," Dom continued. "He ain't *your* old man."

Onorato's shifted his weight. "So?"

"Lemme ask you something, Onorato," Dom said. "And that's quite a name. Onorato. In the old country, it means honored, or worthy of respect. Did your father give you that name?"

"What do you know about my father?"

"Probably more than you do," Dom said. "But let's start with the fact that he's sitting in jail right now for a murder his son committed."

Again, the young man grinned to mask his lack of confidence. "That's crazy," Onorato said, his smile fading. "But I never knew my father. I don't know what you're talking about."

"Your father paid Belinda Smith to stay quiet," Dom said. "He just never acknowledged you. So, you got jealous of his other son. His first-born. Your half-brother, Dion. The pride of the Maggiolis. I bet that was hard, watching him get all the attention. Especially while you were being raised by a single mother. Barely scraping by. No wonder you got into this life."

"You keep my mother's name out of your mouth," Onorato snapped, his eyes flashing.

Dom raised his hands. "No disrespect," he said. "I heard she was a very nurturing, caring woman. I'm sorry for your loss. Truly. I know what it's like to lose someone."

They stared at each other, Onorato's nostrils flaring. Silvestro glanced between the two men while Pauly drummed his fingers on the briefcase.

"So," Dom said, lowering his hands and slipping one under the table, "you're right. The terms have changed. It's now fifty thousand. Each. No fee. Or, for starters, we walk outta here and let Lazaro know about your little—how shall we say—creative accounting. You got it?"

"Ha," Onorato exclaimed, his voice shaky. "I doubt you'd get that far."

"Wanna bet?" Dom pulled out his Beretta, silencer attached, and pointed it at Onorato.

Pauly drew his sidearm, also fitted with a silencer, and aimed at Silvestro. "Don't move."

Onorato raised his hands slowly. "What do you mean 'for starters,' old man?"

Dom focused his gun on Onorato's neck. "I mean, I know a lot more than what I just told you. So, it's fifty thousand each. No fee. Or that ain't the only secret that's gonna come out."

Onorato's eyes darted to Silvestro. "A hundred large, huh?"

"Yeah. We'll make it easy," Dom said. "Let us keep a briefcase and give you the other."

Silvestro drew a breath. "You gotta open it first," Onorato said. Dom nodded at Pauly. Keeping his aim on Silvestro, he reached around and popped the briefcase open, revealing two bags filled evenly with cash. "All right," Onorato said. "Now what?"

"Now you let us walk out with the other briefcase," Dom said. "Your chump at that door lets us go. We walk out, shake hands where everyone can see. We leave. You don't follow us."

Onorato bobbed his head. "Okay," he said. "Slide that briefcase over, nice and slow."

Pauly kept his gun pointed at Silvestro as he carefully latched the briefcase. But when he slid it across the table, he pushed it too hard, and it sailed to the floor.

"Hey!" Silvestro yelled as it landed on his foot. Onorato drew his Glock, pointing at Dom and Pauly who were already in motion. Before he could shoot, Pauly fired at the shelves, shattering bottles of grenadine. The syrupy red fluid splashed Silvestro. Dom charged the table like a tackling dummy, pinning Onorato against the wall as Pauly fired at the seltzers. They exploded, showering Silvestro, who slipped in the foamy liquid and landed in a pile of broken glass. Dom and Pauly, briefcase in hand, bolted for the door. But it wouldn't budge.

"Numb Nuts must be holding the handle," Pauly yelled, trying in vain to turn it.

Dom grabbed the briefcase and swung it against the door. "Open up!" he yelled.

Like an idiot, Nunzio opened it. With a meaty fist, Pauly popped Nunzio in the eye. Dom tossed Pauly the briefcase as they spilled into the hallway.

"Nunzio, you dipshit," Silvestro groaned. "Don't let them get away."

Dom and Pauly knew to split up, separating at the far end of the bar, heading toward the door. The restaurant was crowded now. Not an empty table in sight. Pauly stumbled around the far corner of the bar, trying to stay upright as he lugged the briefcase.

"Dom!" a familiar voice called from a barstool as he ran past.

He turned to look. There was Giuseppina, one arm wrenched behind her back and Onorato's Glock at her throat.

20

"Move and I blow her head off," Onorato growled from the hallway, driving the Glock into Giuseppina's jugular.

Dom froze. With his Beretta still tucked into his waistband, he was defenseless. Giuseppina's pearl earrings grazed her shoulders as Onorato traced the gun's muzzle along the graceful curve of her neck. He pulled her into his wide chest, a hand on the gun and the other on her shoulder. Below the brim of her green felt hat, Giuseppina's fear-filled eyes found Dom's.

"Don't hurt her," Dom pleaded in a low voice. "She's got nothin' to do with this."

Onorato stroked her face. "If she knows your name, she's got something to do with this."

"You sure grew into a brat," Giuseppina said. A gutsy move, but Dom wasn't surprised. "Your mother would be ashamed to see you now."

"Shut up, old broad," Onorato snarled. "Don't ever talk about my mother."

Dom gulped. Forget the money. He'd just lost Florence. And now Giuseppina? He couldn't let that happen. Slowly, he raised his hands. "Let her go and take me instead."

* * *

Where the hallway ended and the restaurant began, Lucky helped Susan up. Recalling her fortune, she said, "You might be right. My name's Susan. We didn't get to that at the wine bar."

He cradled the small of her back, still holding her hand. "Susan, it's a pleasure to finally meet you," he said, scooping up her book, "since we keep running into each other."

She giggled like a schoolgirl, tucking a stray hair behind her ear. "We do, don't we?"

"Maybe the Universe is trying to tell us something," he said with a subtle wink that buckled her knees. He raised her hand to his lips and gave it a soft kiss.

Who said life after fifty was dull? At least men in this age group knew how to treat a lady.

"Maybe," she managed. She was still lost in his eyes when a shout demanded her attention. Pauly was running at them with a gun, chased by a man covered in red splotches.

"Stop!" the splotched man yelled.

Swinging a briefcase, Pauly pushed past them. His pursuer followed, pulling a handgun from his side. Lucky stepped in front of Susan as the man fired. Screams echoed throughout the large space, clearing the bar, and scattering customers across the restaurant. Lucky grasped his arm, which spurted blood. Susan reached for him, but as more bullets flew, he shielded her with his strapping frame. "Stay down!" he ordered.

The man continued to fire, advancing toward the front door. As he sprayed the bar with bullets, glasses shattered all over the floor.

Eight Ball was shuffling dominoes when the gunfire rang out. Eufrasio and Bartolomeo ducked under the table. "Eight Ball," Eufrasio urged, tugging Ottavio's pant leg, "get down."

"Where's Lucky?" Bartolomeo asked.

"The restroom," Eufrasio said, peeking under the tablecloth as Eight Ball crowded in. From his shelter, he saw Gloria Maggioli slide down in her seat. Ubaldo Occhipinti, of all people, guarded her table. Eufrasio's watery eyes searched for his lifelong friend, Fortunato. A pair of leopard print flats hurried past the table, blocking his view. Then he saw two of the triplets from the wine bar, hunkered below their own table. Eufrasio motioned for the ladies to join them. Crawling on hands and knees, they squeezed in with the men. Finally, he saw Lucky, clutching his blood-spattered arm and hovering over the third triplet on the floor.

"*Dio mio!* What is happening?" he asked rhetorically.

***

Lazaro Occhipinti instructed everyone to get down when he saw Silvestro with a gun in his hand. Six men in expensive suits dove to the floor. But Chavonne stood up.

"Baby girl, get down," Lazaro ordered, reaching into his jacket.

"I'm not afraid of my own brothers," she asserted, causing Lazaro to draw back.

"Let them handle this, Chavonne, please," Lazaro said, pulling out a snub-nosed 9mm.

"Like they handled Dion?" she shouted. "They'll fuck this up, too."

Lazaro recoiled. "Chavonne," he urged, "I don't want you to get hurt."

"They're not the only ones who come heavy," she said, reaching up her skirt and producing a slim pistol from a thigh holster. "I can take care of myself."

***

Dom stared at Onorato. "Let her go," he repeated. "Take me instead."

Onorato squeezed Giuseppina's arm tighter, causing her to wince. "Nah, a hostage is good leverage. What use are you to me, old man?"

"I know how Dion died," Dom said calmly. "You want that to get out? Let her go and I swear an *omerta*. On Belinda's grave. It'll stay quiet."

At the mention of his mother, Onorato shifted, loosening his grip on Giuseppina. Dom glanced toward her hat. Her chin dipped slightly, and Dom took a step forward.

"Come on," he said, "let her go."

As he took a second step, Onorato lowered his gun to his waist.

"That's it," Dom said, arms still raised. "Nice and easy."

With his third step, Giuseppina pulled the pin from her hat. In a singular motion, her hat fell to the floor as she jabbed the long, sharp pin into a bulging vein in Onorato's neck. The pin's pearl head came to rest above his shoulder as he staggered. Dom swiped Onorato's Glock and pulled Giuseppina behind him. Then he cocked the gun and backed away while Onorato gagged.

"Don't fuck with old broads," Giuseppina quipped as she dusted her hands together.

Dom's jaw fell open at her crude language, but again, he wasn't surprised. His gaping mouth soon turned into a knowing smile. "You dumbass," he said, watching Onorato sway, blood spurting from his neck. "Young fucks like you always think you're such hot shots. I know. That was me and Pauly before we got made. But you ain't ever gonna be nothin' but a chooch. And mark my words. Your boy Nunzio's gonna get someone killed. You wanna stay in this life, you get him under control. And here's some more free advice, kid. One, don't let someone you don't know swear on your mother's grave. And B, never bet against old age and treachery."

Onorato gurgled, then slid down the wall. Dom put his hand on Giuseppina's back and led her out of the hallway. But before entering the dining room, she straightened her dress and planted a lipstick-stained kiss on Dom's cheek.

* * *

Meanwhile, Nunzio had found his feet. With a hand on his eye, he ran after Pauly. "I got you, Sly," he yelled, trying to focus as he raised his gun. Silvestro was nearing Pauly. He lunged, but Pauly eluded him. Even with a briefcase in his hand, he hurdled a table, like an old rental car ad. But his foot clipped the edge, upending it. He tumbled to the ground then popped straight up.

"Pauly!" screamed a woman crammed beneath a table near the windows. As he turned to look at her, Silvestro ran into the overturned table. Nunzio took aim. But with blurred vision, he didn't see the broken glass littering the floor, and he slid as he squeezed the trigger.

* * *

Gloria's damaged leg prevented her from getting under her table. Terrified, she crouched, pulling her head even with the table's edge as the shots rang out. The noise reminded her of an unhappy home in Staten Island, where arguments frequently erupted and family secrets were protected at all costs. Gunfire was a familiar sound in her neighborhood. But it had been years since she'd heard it at this proximity. Trembling, she let out a soft whine.

"Here," Ubaldo said, turning around. He pulled something from his pocket and tossed it toward her. "This will keep you safe." A silver disk bounced on the table, glinting in the light spilling through the window. She picked up Dion's St. Christopher medal.

"Where did you—"

But before she could finish her question, a stray bullet ripped into Ubaldo's chest, doubling him over. Gloria screamed, clutching the medal as Ubaldo crumpled to the floor.

* * *

Nunzio skidded in the broken glass. A harsh slap skipped off the side of his head. "What have you DONE?" his father screamed as Nunzio reeled, losing his balance again and falling into the glass. Lazaro knelt among the shards, cradling Ubaldo's head.

Silvestro caught up to them. "Zio Ubaldo!" he shouted.

Ubaldo's chest heaved, blood soaking his pale shirt like an overturned inkwell. His eyes fluttered as he struggled to breathe. Gloria Maggioli clung to Dion's St. Christopher medal, tears streaming down her face as she watched Ubaldo's chest fall, rise, and fall one last time.

* * *

"Pauly!" Millie repeated. He ran toward her voice, finding her beneath a table with Margaret and three men. He crouched and recognized Eufrasio, but there was no time to chat.

"Millie? What are you doing here?" From the corner of his eye, he saw Onorato stumbling across the floor. "Wait, don't answer that. Here," he said, pushing the briefcase to her. "Don't let that out of your sight. Stay safe and be ready to run."

Eufrasio waved his hand, signaling that the women would be protected. When Pauly got up, he nearly tripped over a woman who was digging through her messenger bag and peeking around the bar. Then he saw Dom and Giuseppina, whose dress was splattered with blood like Jackie Kennedy in Dallas. Pauly stepped forward, hoping to meet them and walk out the door together. But a pistol in his back altered his plans.

"Don't even think about it," said Chavonne. "Come on." She pressed the muzzle against Pauly's spine, causing him to raise his arms as she pushed him toward her father. Then she pointed the gun at Dom and Giuseppina. "You, too. Let's go."

They convened in the middle of the restaurant, where Lazaro wept over Ubaldo. Onorato wheezed, hanging onto Gloria's table as she looked on in horror.

"Where's the money?" Chavonne demanded, looking at Pauly.

He shrugged. "I don't know—"

"You just had it," she said. "Where is it?"

Pauly smirked. "You think I give a fuck about money? That ain't why we're here, is it?"

Dom took his cue. "Nope. In fact, we got what we came here for."

"Yeah?" Chavonne said. "What's that?"

"My ex-wife, Florence," Dom began as Gloria perked up. "She told me her nephew, Dion, went missing and asked me to find out what happened to him."

"Dion?" Chavonne said, surprised.

"Your fiancé," Dom clarified. He turned to Onorato. "You had him meet you at those buildings at Bel Monte and Collina. Because you knew some things that he didn't. You knew that Carlo Maggioli was in deep with Lazaro. Owed him a lotta cabbage. And you also knew that, in the event of Carlo's death or incarceration, his fortune would only pass to an heir."

"So?" Chavonne asked.

"That ain't all, honey," Dom said. "You wanted that land Dion intended to buy. You wanted him to give it to you for a wedding present. Because it's better suited for grapes than garlic. Then you found out he wasn't planning to give it to you. And you don't like men who don't give you what you want, ain't that right, princess?"

Chavonne twitched, now pointing the gun at Dom. "You can't prove that. And besides, why would Onorato care about what happened to Carlo?"

Dom looked at Onorato, paling as he leaned on the table. Then he looked at Lazaro, still cradling Ubaldo's lifeless body. "Oh, she don't know?" Pauly quietly pulled out his Beretta while Chavonne was distracted. Then he turned toward Millie and nodded toward the door. Dom looked at Onorato again. "You wanna tell her?"

Onorato gasped, "Carlo is my father." Chavonne's jaw dropped.

"You didn't know that your boyfriends had the same daddy?" Dom said. "It's a whole mess. But you know who *did* know? YOUR daddy. Ain't that right, Laz?"

Lazaro nodded, crying as he embraced Ubaldo. Hushed gasps filled the restaurant.

"That's why Carlo got kicked out of the family business," Dom explained. "But Lazaro offered him an opportunity. Take out a loan with him, with the land as collateral. Carlo was so deep in debt he had to rent his family's own land from the Occhipintis. Lazaro knew his secret and was blackmailing him. Now, a lotta local businesses owed Carlo money. The price they'd pay for having him make phony donations and get them some press. And he was counting on all that to pay back the loan. But your brothers, Tweedle-Dumb and Tweedle-Dumbass, put the squeeze on Carlo's marks so he couldn't repay the loan. Then the Maggiolis' land would be turned over to your family. You know, for a sharp cookie, you sure missed some crucial info."

Chavonne shook with rage. "Daddy?"

Lazaro was silent except for a few soft sobs.

"Let's recap," Dom said. "You got mad that Dion wasn't going to give you the land, so you asked your ex—protein shake for brains here—to kill him. But, you hit a few snags. The first was that when you lured him to those empty buildings. You didn't know your uncle was gonna be with him, out for a ride in his Shelby."

"He saw Dion and me scuffling and tried to stop it," Onorato said, his face paling.

"And when he did, he tore off Dion's medal," Dom said. "With me so far?"

Chavonne twitched again as Gloria Maggioli covered her tear-stained face, the medal clutched in her frail hand.

"So then," Dom continued, "your uncle leaves, takes Dion's car, and it's just the three of you. Dion's about to walk the bridge. But Dum-Dum here says he can't do it. He don't tell you why. But you're so pissed you take it into your little manicured hands. You want something done, you gotta do it yourself, ain't that right?"

She flinched at the sound of her own words coming back to haunt her.

"You whacked him in the back of the head in the garage," Dom explained. "I'll give you that. Then you get Onorato to toss him in the back of an empty truck and drop him at the base of the oak tree. When he falls, he hits his head on the roots. If that blow to the back of the head didn't kill him, smackin' his forehead on the roots would. The *colpo di grazia.*"

"That's not … exactly what happened," Onorato said, his voice low. "Yes, Chavonne asked me to kill Dion. Because of the land, just like you said."

"Onorato," Chavonne said, her eyes widening in disbelief, "what are you doing?"

"Well, for one thing, I'm dying," he said. "But before I do, let me set the record straight. I had no beef with Dion. When he started dating you, yes, I was mad. Then I learned he was my brother. I always wanted what was best for you, Chavonne. And Dion was the best man I knew."

Onorato swallowed hard, fighting for breath, then continued. "When he saw us in the garage, he thought we were back together, and he broke it off with you. He was ready to walk out, and I got in front of him so he wouldn't leave. He swung at me. I was defending myself when Ubaldo walked in. He pulled Dion off me. And you told Ubaldo to leave. Dion asked why we wanted to meet there. And I couldn't do it. I couldn't kill my own brother. My father never wanted me. My mother struggled to raise me. And now she's gone. Dion was all I had left, even if he didn't know it. So, I told you I couldn't do it. Dion said, 'Do what?' I was going to tell him the truth. But before I could say anything, you came up behind him and swung a shovel into his skull. He dropped to the floor, out cold. And then you told me to take care of him. 'Put him in the truck and get rid of him,' you said. We both drove to the oak tree, but you didn't want to get your fancy shoes muddy, so you made me give you my boots. You pointed to the tree and then you walked away. You coldhearted bitch."

Chavonne's lips quivered, then dissolved into a chuckle. "You think you can prove that?"

"No need to," came a voice from behind the bar. Kate Kendall stood up, holding her recorder in the air. Chief Novak stood behind her with a pair of handcuffs. "It's all on tape."

"And that's not all," Onorato said, gasping. "You had me sneak around and set up a series of accidents, like the fire at the country club, so it looked like crime was increasing and Dion's death was just another random incident."

Chavonne swallowed hard. Chief Novak studied her face. But Onorato continued.

"And you said that when Dion bought you that land for a wedding gift, you were going to give me half. You'd already convinced him to put you on his account at the bank and you were moving money from it into your savings. You said he'd never know. We could leverage the land in a year or so to one of these chip companies looking to expand operations. You said we'd both be rich and could finally be together again."

It was Chavonne who gasped now, incredulous that Onorato had spilled her deepest, darkest secrets. "How could you—" she began, but Chief Novak was already opening the cuffs.

"Jake," Lazaro pleaded as his golf partner spun Chavonne around, "not my little girl."

But Novak cuffed her and then motioned to other officers who'd filed in from the side door. They arrested Silvestro and Nunzio as a team of EMTs wheeled in two gurneys. Onorato slumped over, collapsing on one of them. As the EMTs worked on him, another crew lifted Ubaldo's blood-soaked body from the ground. Finally, Novak turned to Lazaro.

"You too, my friend," he said, pulling out another pair of cuffs. "Let's go."

Giuseppina came up to Lucky and looked at his arm. She nodded to Susan and then called over an EMT. As Lazaro was read his rights and hauled off, the restaurant began to buzz.

Pauly looked at Millie, then nodded to the door. "Now," he mouthed. Quietly, she took the briefcase, stood, and turned toward the door. Margaret followed, then Susan. Eufrasio, Bartolomeo, and Eight Ball posted like soldiers lining the path. Behind them, the triplets took long, silent strides until they were outside. Pauly watched them turn the corner. Then he turned to Dom. With a flick of his head, Dom implied that they should leave through the side door. With Chavonne raising her voice and demanding a lawyer, the two men backed away and slid out the door just as Margaret pulled up in the rental car.

***

Pauly counted the money at the dining table. "Plenty to get us to our next adventure."

"And to buy me something special," Millie teased. "I didn't forget."

"When we get where we're going," Pauly said. "Wherever that is."

Dom stared out the window, noting the clouds shading the foothills.

"Plane's gassed up," Susan said. "I took care of it before we went to lunch. Whenever you're ready."

Dom barely heard her. Florence was gone. The Occhipintis arrested. Dion, Ubaldo, and probably Onorato, all dead. Sacrificed to this life of cruel circumstances. All to protect the powerful secrets of weak men. It was an endless cycle, and the cash was little comfort. Dom inhaled, letting his breath cleanse what was left of his soul. As he exhaled, his phone buzzed.

"Lucky's going to be fine," it read. "Please let me thank you properly for saving me."

Giuseppina.

"How about you?" Dom texted. "Did they charge you?"

"Self-defense," came the reply. "Besides, it pays to know people's secrets."

Dom touched his cheek, as if hoping to feel her lips there again.

"Still with us?" Pauly asked.

"What?" Dom said, his stare dissolving into a grin. "Yeah."

"We can leave tonight," Susan said.

Dom looked at his phone. "You know what? Let's give it another day or two."

* * *

Before the sun rose the next morning, Dom strolled in the garlic-scented mist. The fog clung to the foothills, but he didn't feel the need for a jacket. Warmed from the inside, he stopped at the corner and bought a humble bouquet of carnations from the man setting up his buckets. When he walked into the café, Giuseppina was already there.

"Good morning," he said, presenting her with the flowers. "For your trouble."

She stood and took the bouquet. "They're beautiful," she said. After setting them on the table, she put her arms around his neck. "But I'm the one who should be thanking you. I don't know what I would've done if you hadn't been there."

When she melted into his arms, he recalled how good it was to hold a woman again. Soft curves and delicate aromas hadn't been part of his life for years. After a long squeeze, he stepped back and pulled out her chair. Once she was seated, he sat down. "You wouldn't have been in danger if I hadn't been there. I bring these situations with me. This life ain't for everyone."

"I see," she said, motioning to the server. A young man with a tray walked up and set a cinnamon-dusted cappuccino in front of Giuseppina. Then he served Dom an espresso doppio.

"Una bella sorpresa, signora," Dom said, a smile blooming as he lifted his cup.

"I'm full of nice surprises," she said with a wink, touching her cup to Dom's.

"So I'm learning," he said, then took a sip. "By the way, Onorato—"

She waved her hand. "Last I heard, he was still in surgery."

Dom shook his head. "That's a shame, gettin' caught up in a mess like that."

"We make our choices. No one forced him to choose that lifestyle."

Dom was silent, reviewing his own life choices and where they had led. Finally, he said, "Please let me pay for this. I owe you for the apple fritters."

"Oh no," she said, setting her cup down. "I owe you, for keeping me alive yesterday."

The sun's earliest beams stretched over the hills, warming the window as Dom leaned forward. "Then maybe, if you don't mind, I could take you to dinner?"

She laid her hand on his and Dom laced his fingers through hers. "I'd like that," she said. "To new beginnings."

He squeezed her hand. "To new beginnings," he said.

"Your paper, Mrs. Rosetto," the server announced, laying a *Town Crier* on the table. But they were locked in silent conversation. The kind that transpires through long looks, quivering breaths, and unspoken thoughts.

OCCHIPINTI FAMILY MEMBERS ARRESTED FOR DION MAGGIOLI'S MURDER IN THE VALLEY OF THE HEART'S DELIGHT, read the headline, by Kate Kendall.

* * *

Eufrasio sat below the madrone on his patio, warmed by the sun piercing the fog. As he unfolded his *Town Crier,* Bartolomeo, and Ottavio joined him. "Good morning," he said.

Lucky, his arm bandaged, followed. He shook a white paper sack. "I can't believe you made me get the bagels, in my condition," he said.

Eufrasio poured each of them a cup of coffee. "It was your week to buy," he said, handing out the cups. "Besides, it's not like you died."

The others laughed as Bartolomeo picked up the newspaper. "Did you see this?"

"Acqua in bocca," Eufrasio said. "Sometimes you gotta keep that water in your mouth."

The quartet nodded in agreement: some secrets were best left concealed.

Eufrasio pointed to a sidebar below the fold. "But this is something," he said. He read aloud, "In a surprise move, Adalgisa Maggioli bought the parcel because, she said, she wanted peace between the two families. The land will be donated to the City, to be preserved as open space in perpetuity. There are plans to build a park, with picnic tables, walking trails, and inclusive playgrounds that can be enjoyed by children of all abilities. The centerpiece of the park will be a fountain, dedicated to the memories of Dion Maggioli and Ubaldo Occhipinti."

They sipped their coffee. "Lovely gesture," Eight Ball said. "Their legacies live on."

Lucky winced as he raised his coffee cup. The others joined him in a toast. "To all those we've lost," he said. "May their memories remain a blessing."

Eufrasio felt the sun thaw his shoulders, casting its warmth across the patio. As their cups clinked, he looked at the bookshelves inside the house, his eyes instinctively searching for Georgette in her bridal gown. Then he turned to his friends. In the sky above Bel Monte Boulevard, a cote of doves alit over the lone oak in the yellow field. With wings glossed by the morning sun, they soared against the pale sky, disappearing into the fog.

ABOUT THE AUTHORS

Donna Lane is a ghostwriter and editor born and raised in San Jose, California. She has been a managing editor for magazines, a newspaper reporter, and online columnist. Additionally, she works behind the scenes as a copy editor and proofreader for a variety of diverse clients and dabbles in graphic design. On an ideal day, Ms. Lane might enjoy a good cup of coffee, pet some dogs, and discuss baseball, somewhere near the water. Creativity is her biggest motivation. A Francophile, she's fascinated by the Jazz Age, loves to cook, listens to several genres of music, and has a special interest in veteran's issues. She is inspired by life's nuances and commonalities that prove we are more alike than different. Donna is a firm believer that every day is a celebration and is happiest in the company of her two adult children.

***

J. Channing lives in Garden City, Idaho. A technologist and entrepreneur, he loves to write fun, engaging stories, from children's adventures and mob comedies to deep science fiction and time travel tales. Born in Butte, Montana, he spent most of his childhood roaming around the northwest, living in eighteen different locations before getting through high school. This gave him a sense of adventure and encouraged his imagination. A student of history as well as technology, Mr. Channing loves to ask, "what if?" When he's not writing, he's an avid water ski and snow ski enthusiast (and occasionally does those two activities on the same day) and loves to ride his electronic skateboard on the miles of the Boise area's greenbelt. Above all, his greatest joy is making his wife and two daughters laugh.

CPSIA information can be obtained
at www.ICGtesting.com
Printed in the USA
BVHW031956300922
648402BV00015B/592

9 781088 063958